I sense your heartbeat. I hear your quiet breath. I lie calm yet deep inside, I rock like a buoy in a restless sea. Your embrace is as gentle as a flower petal floating down a stream. It's a cruel paradox—to be so close to you and so far away, simultaneously.

I waited at the computer, stared at the phone, peered out the window, longing for you. All I wanted was you. You came all this way with a pocketful of romance and a handful of stars. Didn't I pray for cupid's arrows to find their mark? Wasn't that less than an hour ago?

Love aims her bow and I duck and dodge. Walls go up. I'm ice and rock and can't be touched . . . or can I? I'm tired of resisting. What I've wanted all along is for someone to push me through to the other side. To make me want to try love one more time.

Getting There

A Novel by

ROBBI SOMMERS

THE NAIAD PRESS, INC.
1995

Copyright © 1995 by Robbi Sommers

Printed in the United States of America on acid-free paper
First Edition

Editor: Christine Cassidy
Cover design: Bonnie Liss (Phoenix Graphics)
Typesetter: Sandi Stancil

Library of Congress Cataloging-in-Publication Data

Sommers, Robbi, 1950 –
    Getting there / by Robbi Sommers.
        p.   cm.
    ISBN 1-56280-099-X (pbk.)
    1. Lesbians—Fiction.   I. Title.
PS3569.065335G47   1995
813'.54—dc20
                                                            95-14529
                                                                CIP

From your pocket you pull
a handful of glittery rhinestone stars.
"For you," you say.
You spill them across the bed
and then kiss my hand.
A romantic at heart . . .
This book is dedicated to Arlene

SPECIAL ACKNOWLEDGMENTS

Arlene Battishill read and reread this manuscript and offered much help, support, and enlightenment — even when she knew "one last comment" would result in perilous consequences...

And also, Arlene, a thousand XOXOX for the **Woman in Black** — my deliciously dark escort who, with a snap of her fingers, fills the room with fiery serpents and rainbow-hued sparks.

The Big Dogs Who Left the Porch:
Ruby — my firestarter
Dawn Griesman — my wonderful, sweet Hugo
Lisa Correa — my rough and ready protector
Marisa Tonello — my rock-steady dear friend

AND MY MUSE

About the Author

Robbi Sommers was born in 1950. Currently residing in Northern California, she has three sons and works as a dental hygienist. Her remaining free time? Writing, tangoing with her muse, and getting there.

BOOKS BY ROBBI SOMMERS

Pleasures

Players

Kiss and Tell

Uncertain Companions

Behind Closed Doors

Personal Ads

Getting There

Contents

THROUGH AN UNLOCKED DOOR

FROZEN DREAMS

FREE-FALL

THE UNGUARDED MOMENT

THE TAIL OF THE SERPENT

I simply wanted a life.

After twenty years of you-name-it-I've-tried-it, I considered myself a survivor. Desperate years. I whirled into then out of relationships — looking for more, always looking for more. A seasoned traveler with a satchel of fantasies flung over my shoulder, I hitchhiked through romance.

I simply wanted a life.

A life of someday-my-prince-will-come and happily-ever-afters. I had fallen victim to the fairy tales and waited, patient at first, for a prince to gallop into my life and whisk me from the loneliness that haunted me into the sunset. Many princes later, I still sat at the window and stared out to the horizon — gazing at that place where the sun sets and the moon takes flight — waiting, but not. Wondering, but not . . .

And then a door opened and I began a journey to a place I never expected.

THROUGH AN
UNLOCKED DOOR

THROUGH AN UNLOCKED DOOR

The letter came on a day when the gray of winter was overpowered by a sudden blue spring sky. The promise of new hope filled the air. This and her words were an intoxicating mix:

Dear Angel-woman —
When you came into the photo shop today, I felt immobilized, as if my feet were cemented to the floor. As I watched you, an animal wildness surged through

me. My breath quickened. My palms filmed with sweat. All I could think of, the only recourse I had, was to reach for my pen and write. Words poured out of me. The evolution of my love for women sprang forward to you. Everything I knew, everything that's me, leapt toward you, your beauty, the remarkable angel-light you possess.

I had a vision. We were wolves running through a wet, pre-dawn forest together. Yet we had a knowing about ourselves, a logic that animals don't have. A dangerous feeling. An exhilarating feeling. I felt a calling, a challenge, to somehow recount to you how in that mere second, when your eyes met mine, you inspired me. The mystery of who we could be together suddenly unraveled before me — as if one moment I was staring at an empty page and the next, filled with visions, I was sketching a dream.

I saw you and wrote in one breath. You came into the shop and stepped into my world. I looked across the counter and there you were. A thousand lit Christmas trees could not have brought more beauty or more light.

The days of being hooked-in by a wink of the eye or a dazzling smile have long passed. I'm resigned to practicality when it involves *affaires de coeur*. Disappointment and disillusion left me in this place and since then, I've been wrapped in a cocoon of ambivalence. Even so, the romance of these words seemed to sail from the card and embed in my flesh like tiny silver spears. Caught off guard, I simply stood there in a barrage of sudden anticipation.

I reread the note. The scrawled letters tangled haphazardly into one another as if the sender had purposely intertwined them. The signature was impossible to decipher. I flipped the card over. Had she left an inky fingerprint, a typed version of the name, a strand of hair?

This card in my hand was like a burning ember.

I sniffed the card — no trace of perfume. Did I expect that she would indiscriminately pour her cologne across the note like some hopeless romantic? What a flimsy, overdone token that would have been! Subtle. Cool. Nothing too showy, nothing too strong. She'd wear a classic fragrance, an expensive fragrance. Lightly, discreetly, she'd dab it in the hollow of her neck, in the crease of her arm. She was that kind of woman — exact and certain of what she wanted. This card, those words, made that clear.

This card. Those words.

A few days before, I had dropped off film at the women-owned photo lab. Which woman was she? The tall, dark owner with the business-like demeanor — hadn't she looked me right in the eye? The bosomy clerk with the loud laugh — hadn't she said that I made her day? The darkroom worker at the other counter — hadn't she flashed me an unsolicited smile?

One moment I was staring at an empty page and the next, filled with visions, I was sketching a dream.

A writer myself, I'm no stranger to the whimsical nature of inspiration. The fickle muse is both merciless and elusive. When something evokes her, one does not take this lightly.

That excitement of creativity — the words, the desires and everything therein — now simmered inside of me. Which woman had I inspired to reach for her pen and write such words? Which woman had, in some undefined way, inspired me?

It was if each detail in the card held a secret message from her. I studied the picture on the front. Violet-shadowed mountains like a Madonna's veil. *Would her kisses be violet? Her passion the color of thick-purpled wine?* Forest-green trees dotted the otherwise yellow-brown landscape. The terrain was rough — *as rough as her hands on my breasts and my belly? Rough like that?* Across the top, a long, white kite stretched horizontally. An elaborate dragon extended the entire length. Orange-red flames poured from the dragon's mouth, raced down its back then burst into a long fiery tail. Fire — *like the feel of her fingertips lightly caressing my clitoris* — like the sparks that I now felt between my legs.

I deliberated the convoluted signature then peered into the envelope. I ran my finger on the very place where her tongue must have touched — *the tongue that would feel so warm, so silky on my nipple.*

Her return address was in the upper corner. She was expecting a reply? The compulsion to respond was electric. The potentialities were boundless. Maybe this time, love could be different? Maybe this time, I'd walk a path that led somewhere unforeseen? That long-awaited but never reached destination?

Down the block from my P.O. box was the stationery store. I'd find the perfect card, mail it, and in a matter of minutes have fanned an intriguing spark. Maybe we'd meet for lunch. Perhaps she knew a quiet place on the outskirts of town. I certainly did. I knew several. Lunch at the beach. A gray day, a cool day — balanced on a cliff between the green hills and the ocean, we'd cut through the fog. She'd

8

be driving, looking out to the road far ahead. I'd be watching her fingers on the steering wheel.

I glanced back to the card and knew — we should never meet. I'd traveled that journey — fly-by-night love — one minute a tourist on the luxury cruise, Hope, the next tossed overboard to a ruthless sea. Would this be any different?

A card such as this, words such as these were meant to be safeguarded. A romance through the mail. Indestructible. Untouchable. I should simply ask for more letters — a tryst where the players touch with words, kiss with sentences. Launched from a pen, flying across the sky on postage-stamp wings, I'd have all the pleasures and none of the pain.

Mystery Woman (your name?)—

Will you write me more? And more? And even more? When I come to your shop, you could smile. I'd blush and then avert my eyes — and all the while, we'd both know that a treasure chest of words is hidden in my lingerie drawer.

And can you keep a secret? When your eyes meet mine that brief second and I quickly glance away (after all — my heart beats too fast and my face flushes far too easily) will you smile and laugh at our secret and only think of the scent of a sachet-lined drawer?

And are your hands strong from the work you do? Are they steady? As strong and as steady as the words you write — words that are now tucked in a secret drawer filled with satin and silks? And will you keep a secret and write me more? And more? And even more?

* * * * *

I clicked on the night light. Propped against the lamp was my card to her. I hadn't dabbed perfume on the stationery — but this *was* one of those rare instances that a hint of fragrance would have been completely understandable, was it not? Or would she regard my romantic impulse as maudlin? I reached for the card. Across the room, the bottle of Obsession glittered on the antique dressing table.

Many nights I'd imagined the original owner seated on a cushioned stool in front of the vanity's large, round mirror. What fragrant oils did she wear for her lover? Did she smear a teardrop of scent on the letters she wrote? Like I could have done — could still do?

On the wall, catty-corner to the dressing table, was a print by Nagel. The model wore a flimsy blue dress. One strap had slipped seductively off her shoulder and resembled a sea-blue welt on her silvery-pale skin. In the sky behind her, a cool moon hung high.

She had a sense of desolation that pushed yet pulled, repelled yet compelled. It was difficult not to imagine her locked in an endless struggle with her passions. She was an interesting contrast to my lace curtains, my deco furniture, the doilies beneath the pewter candlesticks on the bureau. I liked the paradox, the juxtaposition of hard and soft. My friends sometimes sat on my bed and contemplated the coldness of Nagel's woman, just as I now considered the desire-driven lover (was it 1920? 1930?) who sat at this very mirror and daubed her perfume beneath her recently dried, handwritten name?

I glanced at the Nagel. I didn't envy the icy woman yet something about her snow-glazed eyes helped finalize my decision not to sprinkle Obsession on the envelope. I'm a 1990's woman who's come a long way.

I clicked off the lamp and lay in the dark, certain of two things — Nagel's woman watched me and the moon hung high.

One day for the letter to get to her, a day for her to reply, and then another for the response to find its way to me. Minimum, three days. Would she drag out another day or two in search of a card?

I reread her first letter, again and again. Each time, dreamy sensations and unexpected desires filled me. Because of this, the post office became the focal point of my day. On the way to work, I checked the mail. Lunch hour, I returned. I waited, impatient.

Finally, the fourth day, the card arrived. I ripped into the envelope. A portrait of a white wicker chair enmeshed in a lush, overgrown garden of spring flowers graced the front of the card . . .

My Angel—
Will I write you more?
There's so much more . . .
When I first saw you — your back toward me, your

face turned away, I simply stared. The rip in your jeans, directly below the curve of your ass, held my attention. I struggled to keep moving but instead I stood there and tried, as nonchalantly as possible, to bask in the sight of you.

I let myself go, just for a moment . . . and then I was back — back in the shop, back at the counter, back in life.

You turned — face flushed, hair flame-red. Your pink shirt was partially unbuttoned and your gold necklace drew me to the roundness of your breasts. You looked as if you had stepped out of a dream. I'm not sure if it was my dream or not. It was a dream though, a misty, summer dream, and all I could do was see it, feel it and then just let it go.

How could anyone be so sensual yet homespun? You had a sweetness about you, a charm that countered your innate sexuality. You were perfect. Your lips were a thin, red ribbon. Your nose called forth images of a Grecian goddess. Your eyebrows, remarkably even, arched above your deep, brown eyes.

I stared into you, suddenly forgetting the curve of your ass, the soft indentation of your waist, the fullness of your breasts. Instead, I stood entranced, soaking in the dark sea of your searching eyes.

It was a regular day. A casual afternoon. As regular and casual as seeing a beautiful woman could be. As ordinary as the first spring day. As casual as the full moon, voluptuous and ripe in a tropical midnight sky.

You were admiring the large portrait of vased roses. You stood next to the print and immediately, the roses became secondary to you. Although the

*blooms were exquisite, juxtaposed to you they seemed
to blend into the wall. An abundant sexual energy
swirled in a silent whirlwind around you. The energy
wasn't free-floating yet seemed attached to nothing. It
was simply about you, your being, and when you left,
when the door swung shut — all the air went with
you. You left me standing in a vacuum —
contemplating an elusive dream.*

*You were gone yet something of you remained. I
felt enclosed in a bubble. And quickly, so I didn't
catch myself or have to stop and really think about it,
I wondered about the sudden void in my life.*

*I had no choice but to steal a glance at your
order, memorize your name and address and then
write to let you know how you've inspired me!*

*Beautiful angel — your fragrance lingered in the
air long after you left.*

This time she had printed her name, clear and
precise. *Alex.* I knew exactly who she was.

"Alex, could you have this developed by Friday?"
the owner had asked.

Alex glanced at the owner and then, long and
slow, at me. "Is it an emergency?" She had an
intriguing smile. The intensity of her eyes held me
captive for a moment and then released me.

"Not really an emergency," I said unleashing my
femme charm. After all, I *was* in a room filled with
butches. "I just hate waiting."

"Hate to see a woman like you wait," the clerk
had chimed from the desk.

Alex. The darkroom woman. Her arms were

strong. A confidence flickered in her eyes. She was taller — a few inches — with a stocky build and certain hands. Her close-cropped hair was an autumn potpourri of auburn and gold.

I visualized her and me kissing in the red glow of the darkroom. I imagined her words — mysterious and luscious — whispered in a heated breath.

. . . and there's so much more.

At work, I thought of her. Monitoring blood pressures, taking temperatures, assisting the doctor however I could, I replayed her words in my mind like a lovely melody. To the post office, at the grocery, at home cooking dinner for one — each phrase consumed me. *A beautiful angel who had stepped from a dream. A sweetness. A charm. A rose in bloom; a compelling fragrance that lingered.* Behind the lace veil of distance and abstractions, the possibilities were endless. Everything and anything I'd ever dreamed, in the safety of letters, I'd be all this and more.

Late that night, I wrote to her. Lighted candles brought her to my room. To Elton John's *The One,* we danced in the shadows. With the whisper of blue ink and a feather pen, I called to her, spilling my fantasies across a lavender page.

Dear, dear Alex —
    And would you come in the night through an unlocked door?

With thunder and lightning and so much more?
The scent of desire as your only guide to the
room, to the bed,
where your angel lies
Drunk
Dizzy
Your breath on my shoulder.
Your lips touch my breast and down
and down
and down
as I whisper, "Yes."
I could soar!
I could fly,
an angel am I.
Dare you? Make you? Cross the line
to a dream where strangers are lovers for a
moment in time.
You know the song — one thousand notes
(and lovers are strangers of the sweetest kind).
Would you? Could you?
Steal through the night
through an unlocked door
to an unknown room
to an unknown bed
for an unknown melody of the sweetest kind?
Would you come, in the night, through an
unlocked door
with lightning and thunder and so much more?

The element of anticipation is a delightful, yet cruel master. As soon as I dropped my response into the mailbox, that bittersweet edge began. How long

15

until her next letter would arrive? What would she say? Did she spend her free time thinking of me, of what she'd write next? Did she hurry to her P.O. box as I did mine? Did she? Has she? Will she?

The urge to nonchalantly stroll past the photo shop consumed me. A quick jaunt? A fast pace? A peek through the window and nothing more? After all, I had valid reasons to walk down Fourth Street — wasn't Starbucks three doors down? Didn't I need something from the bookstore across the street? Hell, weren't my pictures developed and ready? Even so, I avoided Fourth. Some days, if it was close to five and there was a chance she'd be on the street — getting in a car, heading for an end-of-the-day cup of coffee — I'd detour well out of my way, dodging any chance that we might accidentally meet.

Oddly, the more I kept my distance, the more intent I became. What if I simply picked up my pictures? I'd be blasé, indifferent. Without a care, I'd casually walk though the door — (A knowing smile? A flirtatious tilt of the head?) — just to see . . . just to feel. We'd be in the same building, in the same room and electricity would snap between us.

Or would she be in some hidden darkroom, watching images appear in the crisp, red light?

Dear Angel —

Before I even pulled the card from the P.O. box, I knew it was from you. A sense of destiny, as rhythmic as the tide, surrounded me. I held the lavender envelope in my hand and momentarily spun in the energy that radiated from it.

Minutes later? Hours later? I opened the card and read, carefully, each delicious word. Like plush petals, each letter slanted in voluptuous curves and sensuous loops.

I thought of you next to those scarlet roses. The memory ignited and burst like a firestorm. A reckless wave of all that you are bombarded me. I grasped the card as if it were a paper raft and hung on for dear life.

Would I come in the night through an unlocked door?

I breathed and breathed and breathed. I sat in the car and just stared at your words and breathed. A treasure, a glittery diamond, a sparkling ruby — your card. You.

Would I come in the night through an unlocked door?

Yes. All this and more. I'll slink down the hallways of your fantasies, steal into your room . . . and with everything I have, lift you from the bed in a thunderbolt.
All this and more.

I lie in bed with her letters and somersault in dreams. *All this and more . . .*

I'm submerged in endless scenarios. I'm lifted from the bed and on a thundering steed. Her determined step, her breath, her heartbeat — down

the hallway, she's coming for me. She penetrates my
dreams and I succumb. For a moment in time, where
nothing counts but this, she has me.

My Alex —
Your angel stares into the star-less night
and waits, anticipating.
And the night is black
as black as the lace she wears
as black as the silk blindfold draped across her
*   bed.*
She aches to be carried back to the place
where safe is the roughness of strong hands
and the softness of sweet kisses.
A stranger
A warrior, ancient yet future
pushes through the darkness
pushes swift, fast, toward her.
From the window, the angel turns
lies across her bed and blinds her eyes in
*   perfumed silk.*
The words, once hidden amongst her lingerie
now lie scattered across her breasts.
And somewhere
far in the night
lightning breaks the dark.

I have fantasies.
A blindfold conceals. I wouldn't see her but I'd

feel her — in the room, near the bed — everywhere. In the realm of fantasy, this I want. This I crave.

I could be hers. Secrets and scents and words of desire — I could be hers . . .

Everywhere. Everywhere. Beneath her strong hands, her soft mouth. I could be hers. In the room, near the bed. I'd feel her desire.

I could be hers with the slick click of an unlocked door.

Passion seeps through black silk and red light ignites a flame. Her breath on my thigh — only closer, yes, closer. My whispers; her sighs — only closer, yes, closer.

Looking for romance. Looking for the pull.

Would she whisk me away — into dreams? Into fantasies?

Would you come in the night through an unlocked door?

I have fantasies.

With her letters close to my heart, I lie in bed, very, very still. Perhaps, if I am quiet enough, I will hear her.

AFTER HER

We were lovers who'd never touched. Letters filled with diamond words were our fingers, our mouths, our lips. Through the mail, we waltzed around magnificent ballrooms. We sailed ivory swans across onyx seas. On a warm tropical beach, she loved me with steadied passion. In a windstorm, she pushed me against cold rocks and had me hard and fast.

We only revealed our fantasies. I had no idea who she was beyond our written clandestine meetings and slippery sex. A romance in the mail — indestructible. Untouchable.

Yet, as the days passed, my inclination to see her — for a mere minute or two — intensified. What harm in a simple peek? A stolen glance? I could only imagine the rush of heat, the fierce tension if her eyes met mine!

Had we not been caressing each other for weeks? Had we not shared the most exquisite adventures? A mere glance, a honeyed smile —

From the bookstore window, I peered across the street. Two exposed rolls of film were in my purse. If that moment came when I stepped out of my body and floated through the doors of the photo shop, I'd be prepared . . .

"I need these developed," I'd say, nonchalantly. Cool as can be, I do a brief scan of the room. She's nowhere. Would she hear my voice? Come from the back just to take a peek?

I place the film on the counter.

"Don't you have some photos here?" a woman — the wrong woman — says.

"Oh my God! I *totally* forgot!" I say, loud enough for a darkroom employee to hear.

And then she comes from the back. A pencil rides her ear. Her fast-blue eyes pierce through me. She smiles and instantly I'm on that beach, against those rocks, dancing to a samba on a sultry, summer night . . .

If only I could force myself — from the bookstore, or the corner of Fourth, or the front of Starbucks, if only I could make my way up that street and through that door.

Had she known all along that I had been haunting her street like a restless soul? Was it a coincidence that the tone of her words subtly shifted

21

until finally the day came when I stood before my mailbox with her proposal.

Would meeting with me cross your boundaries or simply expand them?

Under any other circumstances, I would have dismissed her suggestion to "expand my boundaries" outright, yet my sudden desire to bring life to the fantasy had a momentum of its own — a downhill ride on a careening sled. *Somebody should stop this thing.* This was only supposed to be an affair through the mail — harmless, uncomplicated — every part of me knew this. Even so, I went straight to the stationery store, grabbed a card and as evenly as possible — my hand trembling, my heart thumping — knowing full well that the sled was out of control, I wrote three words . . .

Seeking to expand

I sealed the letter, dropped it in the box and finally, not knowing when the last one had been, I took a much-needed breath.

The letter, a map, and nothing more arrived Thursday.

Dear Angel,
Meet me this Friday at eight
The door will be unlocked . . .

* * * * *

Friday night, I drove to her. The cottage door opened into a candlelit room. She sat, a shadowed silhouette, on a thick-cushioned couch. Without a word — after all, had we not said it all in the letters we had written? — I moved toward her. Candlelight danced across her face. She was even more than I remembered. Her eyes were blue flames, her cheekbones high. Her face was ageless, timeless and the secrets of eternal desire seemed to play on her lips.

I sat next to her and immediately felt as if I were a tiny speck spinning on the point of a needle. Balancing as best I could, I flew in fast revolutions on a sharp edge.

I hadn't realized that the intensity of our written words and imagined trysts had escalated to this . . . Actually seeing her had rendered me weak-kneed.

She stared into me and on impulse, I averted my eyes. Her forearms were thick, her hands strong. A long silence hung in the air until finally her words broke the quiet.

"I want to make love to you," was all she said.

I felt suddenly vulnerable. Make love? Touch? Get close? What had I been thinking? That I'd get in my car and end up at Prince Charming's castle? That this time I would somehow escape the familiar end results? In search of a dream, had I driven myself straight into the lion's lair?

Would meeting with me cross your boundaries or simply expand them?

The force of her presence now spiraled with the words we had written, the fire of creativity we had shared, the passion we had unleashed — there was something about her, about us — that implied so much more.

Seeking to expand . . . in a lion's lair.

I took a slow, deep breath. "I'm very fragile," I said carefully.

Fragile. Yes, I see that. Had she spoken? Were her words riding the air on tiny sprites?

She took my hand and led me to the bedroom. As if prodded by a goddess's whimsical wish or the capricious wave of a magician's wand, I gave in to her.

Since then, I'm certain something deep inside of me has shifted. I'm both distant yet close to myself, tightly bound yet adrift. Her lovemaking has pulled me into a state of perpetual twilight. I stagger, as though hallucinating, in that transitory place where day and night merge. The muffled rumbling of subtle thunder follows wherever I go. An invisible blue-spark trail seems to zip in the air behind me.

She's everywhere.

But what *is* out there waiting through the thunder and past the dusk? What does lie ahead? As if they could somehow protect me, this morning, I taped photos of my ex-lovers on the closet door . . .

From the bedroom window, a heart-shaped prism casts tiny rainbows across the walls. I sense her floating on the multicolored rafts of light. The garden's lavish rose blossoms tease me with the likeness of her fragrance. Her blue eyes seem to peek between leaves of lush trees. A dew-fringed spiderweb glitters and I feel enveloped in the silky weaving of her spell. She works magic, I know it.

I feel her. Like ink stains my fingers, like sex soils my sheets, she lingers . . .

I've mentioned her to my friends, how it's been since that night. Am I drugged? Have I fallen victim to a psychic stupor?

"Like in *The Hunger*," I say, to help clarify my point. "I feel like the physician who, after making love with that woman, feels suddenly different. There was an alien blood in her, and after they'd made love, it was too late for the doctor — hopeless, really."

And of course, my friends simply stare at me with a sort of vacancy in their eyes. I talk in abstractions about a woman, a magic woman I've slept with, but I'm certain they don't understand what I mean. How could they? Doesn't matter, talking seems to diffuse it . . . her . . . Can a drunk sober up by reflecting on her high?

I'm immersed in a crystalline reality. Is it this way for her, too? Has she had a day or two of being consumed? Does she sense me in the shadows, watching from the corners? As she drifts into sleep, does she hear me whisper her name? Does she also see the blue flash of light that crackles and buzzes from her to me? Does she remember my moans of pleasure? How I felt beneath her? Above her? Can she still taste my sweat?

She was so much like twilight, so much like a rainbow. I wander in the mists of her lingering colors. Unable to capture the reds, yellows and blues, my hands sift through the illusion. Does she think of me still? I wonder.

After her, I can imagine making love with no one else. After her, there is nothing but the feel of her touch, the scent of her, the whisper of her breath. I'm caught up in a moment in time, a love story, a kaleidoscope of all that it was.

She wore a gold signet ring on her middle finger. As she was leaving, she took my hands in hers and brought them to her breasts. Traces of my sex cream had dried across the ring's monogram.

She smiled then slipped her hands from mine. A sudden sense of loss swept through me. I wanted that ring on my finger — to somehow wear home a piece of her.

"I want to make love to you," she had said. Her razor-blue eyes incised a thin line across my heart. Was I bleeding? Liquid heat seemed to seep from every pore and I fell victim to a fast, hot flush.

"I'm very fragile," was all I could say.

Fragile. Maybe she said those words. Maybe she didn't — but she caressed my face with one gentle finger and I heard the words just the same.

When a woman offers to protect me, care for me, surround me in tenderness, it supersedes any desire to go slow. She took my hand and led me to the bed. I hardly knew her. I felt vulnerable and apprehensive but didn't say no.

Onto the bed. With a single kiss she drew me out of my hesitations. With a single kiss, a layer of ice melted from me and bubbled into simmering desire on my flesh.

"You!" she muttered, her voice deep. "You! You! You!"

She was one step ahead of me, one step behind. Above me. Below me. All over me. Her desire poured from her and cascaded into me. Waves of who she was bombarded me. She covered me in kisses — thousands and thousands of kisses. Her lips, fast and desperate on my body, sent currents of hard pleasure through me.

I closed my eyes and felt the claws of a panther across my back, the breath of a wild tiger in my ear. Her tongue slashed across my nipples. She was pulling me, dragging me deep into a tangled jungle. Further I slid into uncontrolled places, unnamed territories. Long-guarded boundaries singed then burned.

Her mouth found my navel. She flicked the opening then plunged her tongue into the slit. Again and again, she fucked my belly. A trail of hot saliva criss-crossed my skin. And further, further, further I slid. Whatever she wanted, whatever she did — limits tumbled like fault-line buildings.

Her predatory fingers lunged and my slippery sex, a willing prey, succumbed. I gave way to her. As if I could have escaped her! As if there could have been any other choice but to spread my legs and arch up to meet her!

My clit was engorged with a primitive longing, an

ancient craving. She whipped her fingers in frantic figure-eights across the rigid flesh and oh, oh I wanted her inside me. Sweat dripped from her. She was hot on me, slippery on me. Her fingers pressed against my opened sex. *Let me in. Let me in.* One finger, two, three, then four. With her fist? With her fist? I hardly knew her — a stranger — one moment talking, the next this — with her fist. I raced through an intricate maze of passion and vulnerability.

I was so wet. She was drenched. Would we slip off the bed? Slide into oblivion? Would she give me her ring? Love me forever? With her closed hand, she broke me. With her clenched fist, she brought me down . . .

RAINBOW DANCER

The rain shower presents the inherent possibility of a rainbow. I like this. Every time it drizzles, I wonder if the transitory sun will present its prism of hope. Once, less than a year ago, I was late for work because of a sudden tango between the rain and the sun — the gray day wrapped a hint of sunlight in her arms and swept across the sky. Gray then bright. Gray then bright.

I was cruising down the road when the sun dipped, spraying a stream of gold. And then, in one of those magnificent strokes of nature, an incredible rainbow arched above me. I'm not certain what compelled me — how in one moment I had transformed from a nurse practitioner on her way to work to a rainbow chaser. It's just that, in that second, when I glanced up to see a shimmering veil of yellow, blue, red and green stretched across the sky, something came over me. I was lifted from my life and spiraled into this . . .

The rainbow seemed to beckon, alluding to the direction that I *should* be traveling. I glanced at the clock — ten minutes until lunch hour ended. To the rainbow. To the clock. It was one of those choices. A situation when you know, no matter how you try to force yourself on track, there's no turning back.

The rainbow arced toward the ground, apparently not too far from where I was. If I merely turned left and drove a mile or two down the road, I was certain I'd come upon the place where those incredible colors dove deep into a pot of gold.

Every time I turned a corner, every time I expected to finally reach that elusive place where the rainbow ended, I'd find myself only a short distance more away. Perhaps another corner and a quarter of a mile? An eighth of a mile?

What intrigued me was not the hope of gold treasures. I simply wanted to take off my clothes and run through the colors. I remember being a child, and on those particularly hot days, jumping with glee through a sprinkler's cool water. That feeling — dancing in the color-drizzle at the rainbow's end.

No matter how far I drove, the rainbow was still just around one more bend. I knew this all along; even so, that day, I went for it — chased a rainbow with the dream of dancing in its mist.

* * * * *

Within a month, I was spending all my free time with Alex at her cottage in the country. It was thirty minutes from my work, I didn't care. With her, I slept deeper, awoke refreshed and drove the back roads into town.

Her cottage was surrounded by roses and wisteria. Although the spring was cooler than most, the flowers were more than happy to stretch green promises around the yard. In the garden, sunflowers whispered their awakening. Daisy buds met in thick bunches. Tiny tomato plants doubled in size.

"Move in with me," she said one evening after fierce lovemaking. I was drunk from her touch. Searching for her, I peeked through heavy eyelids. An afterglow of orange and red haloed her face.

Move in? Why not? She had brought me to a place where the next rainbow would surely end.

Not long after, I emptied my apartment and came to dance for her.

MAGIC DANCER

Today I danced for her.

Early in the day she clicked *that* song on the stereo. I was in the bathroom, naked. A constant warmth radiated from the heat lamp. *That* song always has the same effect on me. She knows this. She knows this and intentionally, I'm sure, she played that song this morning.

The music snaked into the bathroom like a thin spiral of smoke. My reflection stared from the mirror, the glass of a picture, the light fixture. Although I was barely five-six, my tumbling curls added the

32

illusion of height. Once told that my profile had the allure of ancient Egyptian queens, I often used dark kohl to line my eyes in a subtle Cleopatra look. I liked this — creating an exotic air around myself.

Queen of the Nile. I smiled and my mirror image graced me with her sphinx-like charms. I felt so beautiful. So sexy. Alone, in the bathroom, I danced to please myself. I luxuriated in my curves as I moved. My hand slowly followed the slope of my breast, my belly and down my hips. I imagined her passing by, seeing me, desiring me like I now desired myself.

As if she could hear my thoughts from the other room, she came to the doorway of the bathroom. She simply stood there and watched as I danced. I felt lost in the music, lost in my sensuality. She has a way of looking through me that sends a vivid sexual impulse careening through my body. She smiled, she followed me with her eyes — God, she plays me like a cardsharp does a strong hand. An electric throbbing beat a constant rhythm between my legs.

I have always hungered for a woman like her. One look and I'm hers. I want her to push boundaries, test limits. Often when we make love, I fluctuate between feeling weightless and hanging on for dear life. She touches me as though I'm Chinese rice paper — so delicate — as if one wrong move would tear me, and then suddenly, she fucks me like I'm a pillow, like she can ram me, blast me, do whatever she pleases.

She gets as rough as she wants, knowing I will never break. Sometimes I'm scared yet it's the fine line that I love. I crave walking the edge between out of control and controlled.

She is an exquisite lover.

She turned from the doorway and I knew exactly where she was headed. I painted my lips with creamy red, darkened my eyes with black shadow and liner and then, eager, I hurried to the wardrobe. I glittered myself in rhinestones, softened myself with lace, contrasted with a leather jacket and sexed-up with thigh-high boots. Who cared that it was only eleven in the morning?

I heard her restart *that* song. When I came from the bedroom, she was sitting on a stool waiting. I felt sleek. I felt mysterious. I let the music come to me, seduce me and then, I began dancing — dancing for me, dancing for her. I can move, oh yes, I know exactly how to move to *that* kind of song.

I teased. I tempted. I danced to please us both. I wanted her to watch, to become so aroused that she could barely breathe. She made no effort to come to me but I felt her soar across the room and grab me, shake me, devour me. Her eyes took in every move I made, and oh dear God, without a single step, she was all over me.

From opposite corners, we made love. I swirled my hips. She didn't move from the stool yet she was at my side, all the same. She has that gift — with a pleased nod of the head she caresses me. I ran my hands across my breasts and it was as if her mouth was on my neck. I pushed my fingers through my long, auburn curls and her tongue was buried against my swollen clit. I visualized my wetness smeared on her lips, her nose, her chin and I danced. I danced. I danced, danced, danced. The scent of sex spun around me like silk thread. Across the room, she sat, patient.

Didn't matter, I could see in her eyes that I had her. I had her good.

With a simple snap, my lace camisole fell to the floor. My nipples stood like hard cranberries. Oh, I can tease. Oh, yes I can. My fingers grazed the burnt-red tips, pinched them, plucked them. I slipped my aching nipple into my mouth and simply sucked — I merely tugged it between my teeth and she was off that chair and next to me.

Not allowing her outstretched arms to capture me, I danced in a steamy circle around her. A trail of rhinestone-fringed fantasies followed each step I took. I enveloped her in all that I could be.

I felt exhilarated. The more I moved, the deeper I descended into another dimension. I had disappeared and the dancer was now channeled from some place way beyond. My dark side, my wild woman, my sister-spirit had come to claim me.

My lover stood, entranced. Like a soul-scorching fire that intensifies in the dark, my dancer flickered and crackled in leaping flames. I watched from the ceiling, from the corners, from the floor. I was separate yet intertwined, all at once. The heat sucked silver beads of sweat from my skin and soon, I was soaked. My leather, my lace, my rhinestones seemed to dissolve and I was left covered only in the illusion of a wild beast's pelt. The image of sexuality, sensuality, erotic power personified itself in me. I was every temptress, every siren, every goddess who had ever lured a great leader to his downfall. I was the intensity of thunder, lightning unleashed, the drumbeat of ancient rituals.

Sex pounded through me. Pressure built,

excitement heightened. I was an atom splitting. I was nuclear fission. I was the beginning and the end. And all of this, everything I had become, spilled from my being and onto my lover.

I saw myself spinning. I was a potent magnet and she, slivers of iron in quivering motion. Waiting was no longer an option, the pull too strong — with a quick jerk, she had my arm tight in her grasp. She led me to the couch and pushed me against the cushions. I smiled then laughed. This was what I had wanted all along. In that bathroom, surrounded by the orange-red heat of the lamp, I had danced for pleasure and now, it gushed from me. My belly tightened. My clit felt heavy and full.

She knows me. She knows me. She knows me. There is nothing like this kind of love. When unspoken words travel through walls. When we touch across rooms. When her concentrated gaze whirls me like a top into her and back to me . . .

She ripped my lace panties aside, lifted my legs to her shoulders and slid her full fingers into my grateful slit. And then, nonstop and constant, my lover brought this magic dancer to her knees once again.

DEATH OF AN ANGEL

With her I said yes. Yes, yes, yes. Armed with nothing but a satchel of words, I climbed on. We planned to ride into the sunset. And why not? Hadn't she come after me? In search of her angel, my warrior pushed through an unlocked door with thunder and lightning and so much more. I had a lingerie drawer full of glittery phrases as proof.

Roses had bloomed all around the yard. Daisies curtsied by the front porch and wisteria flowered, climbing the wooden fence in praise of summer's return.

Through the French doors in our bedroom, I could see Alex on the terrace. She unfolded a lace cloth and covered the glass and iron table. From our bed, I watched her. She was already dressed. Her shirt was a crisp, blue, button-down. The sleeves were neatly rolled halfway — offering me the pleasure of admiring her forearms and hands. The color accentuated her summer-blue eyes. Bleached from the sun, her hair was now lighter than when we first met. Her face was tan. Sunday morning and she looked beautiful.

She disappeared momentarily and then returned with a vase of brilliant, yellow roses. She was gone and then back with a pitcher of juice. The cream-colored china. Two crystal glasses. A bowl of fruit.

Breakfast on the terrace. I climbed out of bed and wrapped myself in a Chinese-silk robe. I tapped on the window. She turned. Smiled.

"I love you." She mouthed the words. And I kissed the cool glass.

We had croissants and fresh strawberries, watermelon that was deep pink and peaches sliced into half-hearts.

"This is so romantic," I said, softly.

"What perpetuates romance," she replied matter-of-factly, "is basic honesty. If we always tell the truth to each other, love becomes impossible to defeat."

If we always tell the truth. These words, which she repeated often over the last few months, created an umbrella of safety around me. With truth as our foundation, how could we go wrong? I loved her for this. My trust in her was unwavering.

"I have searched so long for this." I slid my finger across a luscious sliver of peach. "You please me in so many ways."

I smiled.

She smiled.

After breakfast, we took a walk. Our house was hidden in a grove of trees and often we'd come upon incredible wildflowers growing on the lane. We hiked, kissed against an old oak tree and returned to the house for a lazy day.

She groomed the garden while I sunned. With windows and doors swung open, the music of Bach's concertos floated like playful sparrows from the stereo to where I was cradled in the arms of the protective sun.

Late August, I fell ill. I could barely move. My body ached and my head pounded.

"How are you?" She peeked into the curtained bedroom.

"Sick," I moaned.

"You missing the sun?" She pushed the door open a bit more.

"Yes." My voice sounded young. Sickness had a way of reducing me thirty-five years in age. The past three days, I'd been a five-year-old girl who needed a mommy.

Alex pushed the door further. She held a large

black vase filled with sunflowers. "I've brought you something else." She sat on the edge of the bed and handed me a tiny box. Inside was a golden angel pin. "To protect you."

She squeezed fresh lemons with honey to soothe my sore throat. Restless nights, she caressed my feverish forehead and told me mystical stories of how she'd lift me and we'd fly to an island in search of golden caves and lavish treasures.

Within a week, I was well. Our lovemaking became poetry and art. Her fiery words splashed in vibrant colors across the room. I opened my eyes to see purple, red and blue spilling down the walls to the floor. Her love for me soaked everything — I run my hand across my belly and my hand is purple. I dip my fingers in my sex and they are red. I kiss her and thick blue melts from her lips to my breasts.

She brought me a small brass ball that jingled soft magical notes. She surprised me with more little boxes filled with golden joys — earrings, crystals, beautiful stones. She lit candles and drew hot baths for me. Roses for the kitchen. And for the bedroom, a beautiful wooden angel to hang above our bed.

"An angel to watch over my Angel," she'd said, her voice oh so tender.

The angel's skin was like white porcelain and her hair, jet black. A golden jewel decorated her neck. Outstretched, the angel's wings were an elaborate orange and black. From the moment she was placed above the bed, I was certain she'd always be in flight. By a thin string, she floated. When we made love, she orbited in slow, lazy circles above us.

This is how it was. This is how it should have stayed . . .

* * * * *

Looking for my missing sunglasses, I found the letter tucked under the front seat of my lover's car. The handwriting was bold and certain. The fragrance — lavenders and jasmine? — was difficult to escape. Addressed to my lover, *and only to her,* a letter no longer lay unnoticed in a vacant car. In my hand, this card singed. In my hand, this note scorched.

I pulled the scented stationery from the envelope and then simply breathed. I breathed long and slow. I unfolded the fine linen paper. To my lover, twelve perfumed words . . .

I can only think of you and await your reply — Your Angel.

Her Angel? Her Angel?

I read and reread. Was I standing on the edge of a cliff? It seemed so. I was teetering on a ledge that began with what I then knew and dropped into the bottomless pit of what I would soon know.

Had I been searching for something when I first came out to this car? Was there anything else in the world that mattered now except for this card? *This card. Those words.* Postmarked Santa Cruz — this year, this month, this very week.

None of my business, I reasoned. I slid the letter into the envelope, pushed it back under the seat and slammed shut the car door. I trust her. If this were something . . . if she *were* writing letters to someone . . . she would certainly have —

Would certainly have what?

I yanked open the car door, retrieved that letter and headed for the house.

Carried by a hurricane of fear, I stormed into the house. "I found this in the car." I waved the envelope in front of my lover. "From your *Angel*." The emphasis on *Angel* was jagged and cold.

"From who?" She glanced up from the book she was reading.

What was keeping me from spinning around the room? "Your Angel." I fanned the letter in front of her face. "You know . . . like me. Your Angel."

Alex plucked the letter from my hand and gave it a quick perusal. A floral breeze spiraled then dissipated. "Oh that!" She shrugged as if that letter and this conversation were inconsequential. "A woman from my past. Angela, not angel. I've told you about her, haven't I?"

"You've never mentioned her." I pouted, well aware of the heated relief moving through me. I was more than ready to believe her — more than happy to accept the now-solved mystery of a perfumed letter shoved under the seat of Alex's car. A voice from the past and nothing more.

"Of course I have, baby." She crumpled the letter and tossed it in the wood-burning stove. "She means nothing. Every so often she contacts me. No big deal." She looked me straight in the eyes and didn't flinch. Even so, something was off. Something desperately guarded. A vague shadow in her eyes and nothing more, and yet —

She wrapped her arms around me, pulled back slightly and peered at me. "Don't you trust me?" That shadiness flickered in her eyes.

I glanced at the door. God, dear God. Had we left it unlatched? In front of me, behind me, next to me — suspicion crowded the room. What was that murky darkness in her eyes? What the hell was that?

She cupped my face in her hands. "You *do* trust me, don't you?" Her azure blue no longer held that sliver of dishonesty. Her voice was soft and soothing. I glanced past her to the book she'd been reading. *Conscious Loving* — love based on truth. Of course I trusted her. What was wrong with me?

"I'm here telling you the truth, baby." Her voice was reminiscent of a mother reassuring her child.

I shook away my uneasiness and nodded.

When we made love that night, the angel did not move. Reluctant to conjecture, I chose to close my eyes.

On her desk, her unpaid bills were stacked in a disheveled pile. Her phone bill stuck out from the bottom. *Her phone bill for her private line.* After that night of lovemaking — I don't know why I did it. A sudden compulsion, a momentary urge? — I grabbed the bill. Santa Cruz. Six forty-five a.m. Santa Cruz. Twelve-fifteen a.m. Santa Cruz. One-thirty a.m. . . .

The word *crushed* comes to mind but shrivels compared to the actual rush of sickness that passed through me.

Calls to Santa Cruz while I slept? Calls to Santa Cruz while I lay vulnerable in the next room? A perfumed postmark, Santa Cruz. A voice from the past and nothing more.

I dialed the number.

"Hello?" The woman's voice was as bold as the handwriting on her perfumed note. I pictured a driven woman, a determined woman — taller than me, blood-painted nails and dyed-blonde hair. That kind of woman. That kind of voice.

"Angela?" I said. A thin layer of ice framed the question.

"You must have the wrong number —"

I repeated the number that was printed not once, not twice, but six times on my lover's bill.

"That's the right number . . . but there's no Angela here."

Relieved, I hung up. I slipped the phone bill back in the pile and wondered about fingerprints. Reduced to spying, I felt guilty and ashamed.

She had dozed off by the fire. *Conscious Loving* lay open, face down across her lap. Her legs were outstretched and her feet propped on the wood-stove's brass foot rest. I studied the scuff marks on her boots. Every morning she chopped wood and carried armfuls in before she left for work. Not wanting me to worry about heat on those crisp autumn mornings, not wanting me to worry — she did things for me.

And now, I had to tell her my nasty, nasty secret. Once again, I had crossed a boundary and gone through her personal things. I recalled the day I found the letter under the seat.

"What compelled you to go through my things?" she had said after tossing the perfumed note into the fire.

"I was looking for my sunglasses."

"And that's why you opened a letter addressed to me?" An edge of anger tinged her words.

"Perhaps the glasses had slipped into the envelope?" I tried to lighten things but obviously, at that moment she wasn't interested in my wit.

"You know how I feel about privacy. This is a perfect example of how snooping leads to mistaken assumptions."

"Well, you must admit . . . a perfumed letter?"

"And we have agreements that anything that compromises our relationship, we talk about, don't we?"

I nodded, but she wasn't paying attention to me.

"If this letter, this woman, meant anything, you know we would have discussed it. It was nothing and yet you fly in here like you've caught me in the act of something. As if I'd —"

She had run her hand through her hair. Frustration seemed to surround her in a gray fog. "Please. Stay out of my things. I hate that. I hate that more than anything. It's an intrusion. It's a statement of distrust."

A week had passed since then. She now slept, vulnerable and trusting, in front of the fire. I stared at her, wishing there was some way to avoid telling the truth about what I had done. Gone through her things — sneaked furtively, snooped without regard.

I placed my hand on her shoulder and she stirred.

"Hey." She smiled and then took my hand in hers. "Must have dozed off."

I glanced at her boots. The boots she wore every morning in the rain, across a slippery deck, to insure that I stayed warm.

"This afternoon, I went through some things on your desk." My focus slid to the floor. Shame washed over me. I was telling a dirty truth. "I don't know — one minute I was kind of standing there and the next — well . . . I saw your phone bill and something compelled me . . . I know it was wrong but I —"

She let go of my hand. The book fell to the floor. "You went through my phone bill?"

For an instant, I considered saying that I hadn't looked. But I knew our agreement — honesty came first. "Yes." I felt as if warm mud was creeping down my face.

"Because why?" She stood up. "Because you don't respect my privacy? Because you don't trust me? Why?"

I shrugged. I had no answer. I braced myself. This was only going to get worse. "I called the number to Santa Cruz."

"Oh Jesus." My lover crossed the room. "Did you speak to —"

"No, it was —"

"Angela called a few weeks ago," she interrupted.

She continued as if unaware of my involvement in the conversation. "She was in a crisis. I helped her through it. Bottom line, when the chips are down, Angela knows she can count on me as a friend."

"That's Angela's number?"

Apparently not listening, my lover was on a tirade. "Any other questions, Miss Snoop? Any other things you've done to prove to me you can't be trusted? Shit. Shit. Shit. Shit. Going through my things. What next? What the fuck next?" She grabbed her coat and stomped out of the house.

Confused, I stood by her empty chair and stared at the wide-open door.

That evening, when I searched for her phone bill, it had disappeared. Not in the pile, not in the desk, not filed with her paid bills — it was nowhere to be found. I no longer cared that I was intruding on her privacy. I no longer cared about anything except for finding out the truth — was she a liar?

Resorting to subversive tactics, I called the phone company and said I was her.

"I've lost my bill," I said, innocent, businesslike, cool, "and need the Santa Cruz number on the bill."

Mother's maiden name? No problem. Social security number? No problem. Within minutes, I had that slippery, slimy number in my hands.

"Hello?" That same voice. Oh yes, I remembered the certainty, the boldness, in that voice.

"Yes, I'm calling for Angela, " I said, more bold than her, more certain than her.

"Wrong number."

"Wrong number? This isn't Angela?" I repeated the number.

"Right number. No Angela."

"No Angela? Are you sure?"

"This is the Flanders residence and there's no Angela."

Did she lie about the name? Is she having an affair? Does she call from a pay phone and pay with cash? Am I caught up in trust issues like she says? Am I blowing things out of proportion? Why does she lock her briefcase in the trunk now? Where does she keep her car keys? Her desk is clear. Her life has become a blank page.

I have become a love terrorist. I call Santa Cruz late at night and then hang up. I think about my ex-lovers and want to be held long enough to feel safe. I regret having taken the pictures down from my closet door. Had I left them, maybe I would have been protected from all of this.

I'm spinning in turmoil. Am I sleeping with the enemy? Am I caught up in a vortex of self-sabotage? Alex says I'm engaged in "self-destructive tendencies" — that our intimacy has become too much for me so I'm subconsciously out to destroy it. She wants me to see a therapist.

Last night, while she slept, I found her keys in her shoe. I stole out to her car, opened her trunk, went through her briefcase and found it — the sealed letter to Beverly Flanders. Santa Cruz.

In the dark, cold and alone, I peeled it open.

My dear Angel — I will call you as soon as possible. The work phone has been cornered and time is so short . . .

She's a liar.

ACTS OF TREASON

"I think she lies." I can't seem to pull my concentration from the stream of light pouring through the therapist's window. This seems to be the only safe place left in the room.

Alex's disapproving sigh breaks the silence.

"Have you lied?" the therapist asks my lover.

"I don't lie," she replies, not hiding the belligerence in her voice.

I glance at the therapist who's looking intently at Alex. "Your story does sound a bit convoluted."

"Since when is having an old friend convoluted?" Alex hisses. "A friend who I'm certain wouldn't snoop through my things. A friend who trusts me." She glares at me. I glare back.

"Oh, please," I say, not hiding my irritation. Was she simply going to turn this around, yet again?

Alex hesitates momentarily and turns to the therapist. "As I said, Angela is an old friend." Her tone has softened. "She had been having a hard time with her teenage son and called me for advice —"

"Her name's Beverly, not Angela," I interrupt.

"What happens when someone snoops, when she goes through other people's things —" She shoots me a covert, sharp look. "— is that information is taken out of context and therefore misconstrued. If there was someone else, why would I even be here?" She smiles smugly

"About Beverly and Angela —" The therapist takes control. "I'm confused here. There's the letter to Beverly . . . who you call Angela but she doesn't answer to Angela when someone telephones. You addressed the letter to Beverly, but write, 'Dear Angela,' which looks like Angel, but you say is really Angela?"

"Yes. Exactly." Alex shrugs. "Angela is Beverly. Well, actually her middle name is Angela. She never liked the name Beverly and so —"

"When I called her number, there was no Angela there." I snap. 'Beverly,' she says. 'No Angela here.' She had no idea what I was talking about. Beverly. The same Beverly that you addressed the letter to — the letter to *your new angel*." Those last words leave a bitter taste.

"Beverly is protective of her privacy," Alex says to the therapist. "She only answers to that with me. She's just a friend. Certainly not —"

"First it was letters to me — *your angel* — now it's letters to her. Why must you lie? Why can't you simply say it! If you want her, fine — just tell me the truth. This makes me crazy. Basic honesty — isn't that what you've said. Yet you lie. Why?"

Alex gestures to me. "You know that our love means everything to me. How close you are to my heart. You are a rose and —"

I stop listening. I know by now how clever my lover can be with words. Isn't that the very thing that drew me to her — her glittery, gem-quality phrases?

We were wolves
Running through a pre-dawn forest
A dangerous feeling.
An exhilarating feeling
The mystery of who we could be together
suddenly unraveled . . .

"Your trust issues are hard on you aren't they?" So many times she had said this to me, her voice so sugar-sweet. In her arms, she held me like she'd protect me from the harsh, cruel world. "I'm here telling you the truth, baby." The tear on my cheek was rescued by her warm fingertip. "This is the one thing you must believe."

Masquerade. Charade. Her stories of why and where made less and less sense. *Your trust issues.* Survivor. Nobody's fool. I found out. I found out. I'd wait for her to fall into sleep and then look for evidence — in her briefcase, in her car, on her phone bill. Reduced to this.

A silence grew. Less a lover, more a double agent. Asking questions with ulterior motives. Checking up, finding out. Sneaky. Slippery.

Over the weeks, I've gone through her things, followed my leads and now, I'm hot on her trail. I've confronted her and she's worried. Across the room, she spins her same old story to the therapist. Her fast-talk disgusts me.

From best friend to false friend, my lover has drifted like an unreachable kite far above the sea. I'm sleeping with a lie. Living with a lie. I've sorted through her wallet for clues. I'm stacking them up.

"I'm not a liar," she repeats.

Con artist. She looks me straight in the eyes. She unclenches her fist — the very fist that once pushed its way deep into me, the very fist that forced me open only to bring me to this vulnerable, aching place. Her hand is outstretched. I expect tar-covered gems to fill her palm but there's nothing, absolutely nothing.

"*Her* trust issues are what we should be scrutinizing," she says in that slippery voice of hers.

I stare at the stream of light and consider escape . . .

. . . I want to kiss my ex-lover again. Yes. Sneak out of this stuffy room, jump in my car and head

west. I know where I'd find her. She's one phone call away. She's waiting for this moment — she told me this. Perched like a mountain lion ready to lunge, she knows how I get when I'm looking to survive. She knows how I feel about liars . . .

. . . Alex rambles on and the room seems to fill with crinkled dead leaves. I can't breathe very well. I need to grab the keys and take the car. Fast. Eighty-five or ninety, down the freeway, I'd be racing toward relief.

"She kissed her ex-lover two days ago and wants to kiss her again." Alex's accusing voice pulls me out of the car and back to this airless room.

Both she and the therapist are staring at me.

"You've kissed someone else?" the therapist asks.

A tight tension shoots through me. "Yes." I can barely stay in my seat. I want to start screaming. The urge to stand up, stomp across the room, grab Alex by the throat, overwhelms me. *Don't you see what you've done to me?* I'm yelling at her but the room is silent. *Late at night — for how many nights? — I wrestled with my intuition like it was a demon to be silenced.* "And yes. I want to kiss her again. At least my ex tells me the truth." I glare at Alex. "I've had it with the lies. I've told you this again and again. But it just goes on and on — don't you see I have nowhere to turn?"

I scan this stifling room and wonder in which corner the last bit of oxygen is hidden. Will I simply collapse right here? I gasp for air. It's so hard to breathe anymore.

"Are you trying destroy us?" Lightning words flail from my lips. "Are you?" I jerk from the chair and move toward the beam of light. "Does this please you in some way? Gaslighting me? Making me feel so crazy? *You* always insisted on honesty. 'Stay in the truth,' you say —" I run my hand through my hair. I want out of this room. Out of this town. "Do you think it was easy to tell you I was going to kiss someone else? To stay in *that* truth?"

This feels hopeless. I turn away from them to stare out the window . . .

Back in the car, I'm looking for the exit that will lead me to a phone. I could meet my ex-lover soon, wherever she says.
Please. Please.
I'm sleeping with a soul thief. I'm negotiating with a weapons vendor.
Please. Please. Please.
I'm just looking for someone to tell me the truth.

"I tell you every fucking thing!" Tears are streaming down my cheeks. "All I want is for you to be honest with me. This makes me crazy. This makes me sick. Anything you say, anything you are, is okay — just tell me the truth."

"I don't lie," my lover insists but she's looking at the floor.

"Swear. Swear on our relationship." I'm desperate now. This is it. We both know that words of honor, falsely spoken, eventually return like flaming boomerangs.

"I swear on our relationship that I have never lied to you."

And there it is.

I've never felt as empty as I do in this moment.

There's nothing left.

Except . . .

to get to my ex-lover as soon as I possibly can.

ON THE LAM

One phone call to her and I'm a fugitive. An escapee, I duck and dodge until I get to the park. Twelve forty-five. We're meeting for lunch, or so we say. I know and she knows — this rendezvous has nothing to do with food but everything to do with filling up.

I'm so hungry that I can barely see the road ahead. The windshield appears covered with rain, but the sky is clear and bright with sunlight. Tears spill from my eyes, down my cheeks. I am so, so desperate. I'm starving. Through the gates and into the park, I'm on my way.

Burdened by betrayal, I climb out of the car. Weary from my paradise lost, I walk toward her. She's leaning against her truck. She looks as good as ever. Her jeans are tight — and oh, yes, I remember the strength of her thighs. Her tank top reveals her muscular arms — and oh yes, yes, I remember the intensity of her embrace. Dripping with that same bravado attitude that held me hostage for that year or two, she doesn't move. My pace is slow. Determined.

Each step takes me further from the grief or closer to self-destruct? I peer past her to the pearl-blue sky, half-expecting a blazing boomerang to cut through this moment and plummet like a burning bird.

Oh God. Oh, oh God.

"You look so good," she says and for a second I wonder if she's lying.

Who tells the truth anymore?

I'm almost there. Will she spare me the anguish of that first, excruciating move? Will she reach for me, take me in her arms and kiss me once again?

She pushes her fingers through her short hair, smiles that devastating smile and then extends her hand. "Really. You look so, so good."

Over the wall, making a break for it — I'm on the run. I won't look back. There's only forward now. We stop on a deserted country road. She hands me a fifth of tequila and I take a swig from the bottle. She

She wants me to get high. The strength of her conquest depends on how far I'm able to escape from myself. We both know this.

A slow-dance in the center of a back-country road. In her arms, I'm no longer connected to the pain. In her arms, I'm a tourist on an extensive cruise from despair. In her arms, I am safe for the smallest, leanest moment in time.

She holds me.
She kisses me.
She's all over me — but something unexpected
something worse than I can imagine —
happens.
In her arms, I feel nothing.
Absolutely nothing.
Have I turned to ice? Have I?
Will I melt from her heat only to disappear?
Nothing.
On the side of the road and down the hill, she
    lies on me and whispers my name.
Kisses me. Caresses me.
Nothing. Nothing. Nothing.
My top slips off. My pants are pulled past my
    thighs to my ankles. We're naked in the grass
    and I feel nothing.
She squeezes my nipples.
Nothing.
She traces her tongue down my belly to my clit.
Nothing.
On the run, over the wall, I'm escaping as fast as
    I can
into nothing.
And after this —

I go home
tell the truth
leave my lover
and not look back
ever again.
A thousand miles ahead of me
and I'm walking aimlessly down a country road
feeling feeling
nothing.

LABYRINTH

All this talk about love-ever-after —
I'm not going to love anymore.
After this second, my love for you melts into the
cement and disappears for good. You brought me
here. You grabbed me by the hand and pulled me,
shoved me, prodded me down this long corridor. I
stumbled down dim-lit hallways, hurried around
maze-like walls, raced the dream of ever-afters while
you ran ahead, spilling flower petals on polished
floors.
Here I stand, stuck in some makeshift dead end,

cornered in some unexpected place while you spin
your lies to some other girl.
Liar.
Liar. Liar. Liar.
"Tell the truth," you said. "Only tell the truth."
Liar.
Those ace-of-hearts words you dealt are spread
across my bed.
"Put it all in the pot," you said. "Give me all
you've got."
Bluff or no, I can't compete — playing poker with
a vulture. Shady. Slippery. Cardsharp deals. I know
about you now. I know how many aces you've got up
that silk sleeve. You hide behind your fake-diamond
cufflinks and your fool's gold eyes.
Flashy.
Splashy.
Slick as oil.
I know about you now.
"Tell the truth," you said.
And I did — again and again I told my truth
while you cast pretty petals on polished floors. Tap
dancer. Snake charmer.
I slip and slide across your lies
and break and shatter
and say
No more.
Done.
Tangled in your maze of lies
a helpless fly.
No more.

FROZEN DREAMS

FROZEN DREAMS

Will the numbness ever dissipate?

I've come through the other side of a broken heart. I've walked across burning coals, leapt from precipices without thought, stared into mirrors and wondered why the endless tears weren't blood.

With you —

I was a beautiful bird. I trusted you implicitly and feared nothing. Soaring high above, I floated on the warm current of possibilities.

From somewhere unseen, somewhere below, a deliberate arrow raced gravity, challenged the odds, finding its mark in my tender heart. A deadly hit. A mortal wound. There was that moment when I searched for you, certain to see you circling below, arms outstretched. The blinding pain was overshadowed by absolute disbelief. As I tumbled in unending circles, I spotted you stealing through the brush — dressed in camouflage, empty bow in hand.

You.

You were my last hope. The end of the line. Isn't that what I told you, again and again?

"I'm fragile," I whispered.

"Yes, yes." You took my hand and pulled me in close. Your crystal-blue eyes hinted nothing of the deadly dagger tucked in your belt. Your silky words were the stiletto's sheath.

The end of the road. A bird once soared high above. Wings outstretched, dazzling those below with the suddenness of orange and black and all the while, the hunter stalked, bow in hand. The arrow slices into my heart and I catapult to the ground without hope.

I fall fast — spiraling in the dismay of frozen dreams, twirling in quick-sand promises. You led me to a gilded door that dropped into a desolate cave. Dropping, spinning, I feel all that I know myself to be collapse. While you — concealed in dark green and beige — blend with the forest. There's no trace of you where I'm going now.

The earth flies toward me and I tighten, toughen, prepare for impact.

The closer I get to the hard ground below, the more numb I become.

TODAY

She came over today with three scarlet roses and a card filled with words about love lost.

"Come home," she pleaded. "Please, please come home."

She held me like she used to. Her eyes were as blue as the Pacific, as blue as the huckleberries we picked last spring, as blue as the wisteria that hung on the front gate of where we lived. In her eyes, I saw the ancient warrior, the wolf, the panther lurking behind blue-cloud veils.

For a moment, today, I forgot about the pain and

only remembered how I soared like a bird at daybreak from where I was to her, how like a raven she came through an unlocked door riding thunderstorms and so much more. Had I simply been struck by lightning, my life would have been easier, made more sense.

I'm balanced on a tightrope. Eyes clenched tight, I move across the sky on a thin wire — a thread-like, razor-sharp wire. Today.

Today she was on the doorstep with a bouquet of memories. Like the flowers that once filled her arms, she brought reminiscences of petal-soft kisses, of scarlet-hued words, of long-stemmed promises. "I'm sorry," she whispered, but her words seemed to evaporate as quickly as they were spoken. Everything she said was suspect.

Was a sliver of darkness tucked discreetly behind her clear blue irises? Could I ever believe her again? Somewhere deep inside, a door had slammed shut.

Liar.

Trapped in a blackened room
liar
far, far below where she now stood
liar
I was crouched in a corner, crying.

She turned to leave. With her, tucked somewhere in her black satchel, was all the hope. I felt no compulsion to reach for her, for it, for anything. Something was dead. I had no more illusions about romance. As much as I knew I would mourn this loss, for perhaps a lifetime, I had no choice but to watch her go. She kissed me good-bye, then disappeared.

I stand, stunned and staggering. Emotional

desolation moves through me, cold and deadly as a sleeper-waved sea. From the window, I stare at the moonless night sky. I can barely see; even so, I sense a crow circling somewhere above.

Restless, I stumble to my car and head for the dark Pacific. The ocean rushes toward me, tempts me, calls me. Scared but not, I weave like a numb drunk to the wet, cold mother. Sand sifts through my fingers and a jagged hole is all I have to remind me where my heart once was.

Like spring touching barren earth, she was inside me. The ocean is blanketed in heavy fog, huckleberries lie withered on a forest floor and wisteria hangs limp on a thirsty vine.

Tonight, I stare at the vacuum where the moon once graced the sky and wonder why freedom feels so tight.

FREE-FALL

NO ILLUSIONS

She was arranging a spring display in the large window of the flower shop when I walked by. Her back was toward me, but I was certain who she was. The new butch in town — I knew about her, every femme knew about her. She lifted weights at the gym, worked at the flower shop and ate lunch alone at the bookstore café.

Her jeans fit tight around her curved ass. Her build was strong. The first day of spring. Wouldn't a bouquet of daisies look nice on my bed stand?

Three shops down, across the street was the photo

shop. Several months had passed since I had even walked down this street. But spring was in the air and I was emerging from a cocoon.

The florist placed the last bunch of daisies and suddenly turned. She smiled then climbed from the window. My heart began to race. Wasn't I a butterfly? Hadn't I, just this morning, decided that freedom no longer felt tight? That I could go where I wanted, do what I pleased? I pulled open the door and walked in.

She had disappeared somewhere beyond the daisies, past the daffodils, in through the roses . . .

The rose was deep red. I teased my finger between its cool, velvet petals and into the plush, soft center. Seductive as scarlet silk, creamy as expensive satin, the yielding crimson flaps spread sweetly. The delicate petals flirted — soft against my finger, smooth against my finger — implying the pleasures yet to be revealed. I stirred my finger slightly and the rose responded with the gift of its piquant fragrance.

"Heart's Desire."

From behind me, a woman's direct voice sent a steel-gray guilt rushing through me. I quickly slid the flower back in its bin and fanned the neighboring roses around it. Had she seen me fondling the rose? Seen me with my finger buried deep between the petals? Was she thinking, "Dear God, where do these floral perverts come from?" Cornered in the back of the florist shop, eager to shield my incriminating finger from scrutiny, I stuffed my hand in my coat pocket, took a fast breath and turned to face my fate.

"Excuse me?" I mumbled.

"—that particular rose. It's called Heart's Desire." The woman from the window skimmed her fingertip across the rouge skirt of the same rose I had been holding. "It's one of my favorites." She gently rolled one rich petal between her fingers. "It's a hybrid tea rose. Interesting fragrance. Almost peppery." She brought her scent-smeared finger to her nose.

She was slightly taller than me, maybe five-six, five-seven. Her dark hair was short on the sides but long enough on top to be brushed straight back. I liked the way her pale green eyes were framed with thick lashes and strong brows. A pencil was tucked behind her ear and her shirt sleeves were rolled up. A woman who meant business, no doubt about that.

"That shade of red has romance written all over it, wouldn't you agree?" Her willow eyes twinkled. She pulled the rose from the bin. "Can I get you some?"

Could she get me some? Uncertain if she was offering flowers or romance, I reached for the rose. A gold band flashed blatantly on her pinkie. Was there a woman somewhere across town wearing that same band? A trusting lover who had, just this morning, kissed this florist good-bye?

I meant to hand her back the rose, to say no thanks to the flowers or anything else she had to offer but instead, I simply stood there nodding my head.

She pulled several more roses from the bin. "Will a half dozen do it for you?"

Her arms looked strong, her hands determined —
two qualities that endeared a woman to me, right off
the bat. Had I thought her eyes were pale? On
second glance, they were lustrous, glimmering with
possibilities far beyond a simple bouquet. *Would a
half dozen do it for me?* I flashed her a sweet smile.
What *would* do it for me was a couple hours alone
with her. Hell, a half day with her. We'd go for a
ride, far up the coast, where nothing counted but the
moment. I pictured us hiking across a field. She'd
lead, I'd follow . . .

We tramp through a never-ending sea of
thigh-high mustard flowers, deep into a dream of
vibrant yellows and greens. She throws a blanket to
the ground and flops onto it. A flurry of tiny gold
petals sprinkle from the protesting flowers. She tugs
my leg and down I go. The sky stretches like a
cornflower blue canopy above us. Industrious bees
hum as they race toward their ecstasy. I know how
they feel. I know all about nature's pull.

The sun is fierce, so fierce that even the bill of
her baseball cap can't shield her face from the heat.
Perspiration beads on her forehead and trickles down
her neck. I imagine her slippery, damp body sliding
on mine. I want her. I want her right now. Hidden
in a circle of green, there's no one to witness but the
nature-driven bees.

I don't care about the gold ring — most probably
too tight, too constricting, on her pinkie. I don't care
about what happens when she leaves me at my car.
Right now, I am desperate for her to press her
sweat-slick breasts against mine. She kisses me and
her dampness smears on me. The mustard, the air,

the earth bring their scent to hers — entwining, weaving, until the fragrances twirl in a delicious spiral. I'm a little breathless . . .

"A half dozen is fine," I muttered.

"Anything else?" She looked me straight in the eyes.

Anything else? Anything else? No . . . unless . . .

In the field, on the ground — she pulls off her T-shirt. I tug off mine. For a moment, she blocks the sun but the momentary shade does little to cool me. Like summer dew, sweat glistens between her breasts. Will she come to me? Slide on me? Grace me with such pleasures?

She leans over me. Droplets shimmer on her face then drizzle onto me. I am so wet between my legs, so spicy wet.

And down, like a waterfall in slow motion, she cascades onto me. Her breasts are soft. Her nipples are hard. Warm, squishy dampness is all that separates us. When she fucks me — oh God, please, *if* she fucks me — she'll be white lightning across my belly. She'd lie on top of me, this I know. She'd lie on top of me and penetrate me all at once. Fuck me like that. Fuck me just like that. She'd glide on me, fly on me, race us into blazing bursts of orange-red fire . . .

I glanced at her ring then shifted my attention to her eyes — those tempting, cool, cucumber-tinted eyes. The gold band's implications began to fade. I considered rolling in a field with a good-time gal, heading for a place where the moment doesn't count.

"Anything else?" she asked again.

Suggesting that someone, somewhere, was pursuing my heart, the roses added a lover's ambiance to my living room. Like crimson hummingbirds, the blossoms seemed transitory, elusive, as if they had alighted on the unadorned stems only moments before and, in an instant, could flutter out the room, far from reach.

Ten dollars a rose. Could have seen a matinee seventeen times. Could have filled my car with gas, six weeks straight — bought groceries for the week, electricity for the month. In the back of the floral shop and alone with her, unable to escape that hammering thought — *those thick fingers of hers pushed in me* — I had pulled out my wallet and done the deed. Jesus. Sixty bucks for six roses. I plopped on the couch, propped my feet on the coffee table and stared at my elaborate expenditure.

And for what? Had she thought that I was swept in a courtship and buying them for my girl? *Sixty bucks for six roses.* Did she think I was in the midst of a blazing *affaire de coeur*? *Sixty bucks for six roses.* Had she even the slightest inkling that I'd bought the roses simply because she looked so good selling them?

I pulled a single rose from the vase. Each petal offered little resistance as I plucked it from the stem. *She loves me, loves me not. Loves me, loves me not.* Petals sprinkled on my lap. Ten dollars a rose. Twenty-five, thirty cents a petal? *Loves me. Loves me not. Loves me.*

I recalled those seconds? — minutes? — hours? in the flower shop with *her* at my side. Her fingertip slid across the rose's satin skirt. Her eyes suggested plunging into a sea of petals. *Anything else?* she had asked. *Anything, anything, else?*

Promises wove in thin gold strands between her shimmering words. And no, there wasn't anything else I needed, not really. There was nothing that she, nor anyone, could offer that wouldn't soon mutate to a parched version of what it was meant to be. Velvet petals soon crinkle and dry.

I had no more illusions about romance. Unlike my friends, I didn't dream about it, pray about it, plead, cry or whine about it. It was simple. If someone sent flowers, lit candles or bought me a gift, I'd take it for what it was — a nice time, a sweet gesture, a momentary attempt to reach impossible heights. But I knew, all too well, that everything fizzled when reality stepped in.

I reached for another rose. Pluck, pluck, pluck. She loves me, loves me, loves me. Petals piled in a sex-red mound. Pluck. Pluck. Pluck. She would fill my empty hot tub with deep-red petals. Naked, I'd step in. Naked, she would follow.

She is gentle with me at first, as gentle as the silky flowers feel against my skin. Her kisses are sugar-spun. So slight, so sweet, she calls me to her with her tender lips.

She embraces me and I float in liquid rubies. Aroused and aching for more, I kiss her with intention. My nipples stiffen as my tongue finds hers. Slowly, seductively, I brush my breasts across hers. Immersed in petals, swimming in petals — hundreds and hundreds and hundreds of petals — I'm flirting, a mischievous sprite.

My nipples kiss hers. Back and forth, so very lightly, I dance, dance, dance. My nipples taunt. My nipples tease. It's too much and not enough. She grabs me and kisses me rough — as if we've run out of time, as if, if she didn't have me this very second, she would cry out in despair. She's determined. She knows what she wants. She pursues what she needs. Backward, into the ocean of roses, I stumble. Down. Down. Down, I sink. Perfumed petals cover my face. All I can see is endless red. On and on, red, red, red. Each breath fills me with the spicy fragrance of Heart's Desire. *Peppery,* she had said. Peppery like sex can smell. Peppery desire.

Buried in nature's velvet, I am hers. Ready for whatever she has. Let her sink her mouth onto my sweet-tipped, pink flower. Let her rim her fingers across my petaled flesh. Welted and rippled, bulky as any flower-enfolding bud, my clit could be hers with the pluck of her thumb. Her strong hands clasp my thighs. Her nails press hard into my flesh.

All I can think of, all I can consider is the thickness of her fingers — the thickness of her fingers and the tightness of my cunt. Through the curtain of flowers, I blindly push my hand to my sex. My pussy is wet. My pussy is drenched. There'd be no problem squeezing one hefty finger into my saucy cunt. No problem at all.

Submerged in a potpourri of passion, I grasp for her hand. I shove it. I shove her hand to my pussy and guide her fingers to my slippery slit. The pounding in my chest leaves no room to breathe. I gasp for air. Pant for air.

Pulsating, churning — I want more. I ram her and jam her as best I can. Her fingers — her ungenerous, stingy fingers — refuse to penetrate. She flattens her hand against my greasy opening but does not budge. What a cunt-tease she is. How exasperating!

I won't take this torment a second longer. Petals fall aside as I sift through the pool of velvet, to the air, to her — I beg her for more. I'm perched on her fingers, trembling on her fingers —

"Oh yes!" And she plunges.

"Oh yes!" And she thrusts.

"Oh yes!" And she fucks me again and again . . .

Pluck. Pluck. Pluck. Fluffy torn flowers were scattered across my lap. Thirty cents a petal. Ten dollars a rose.

When I flirted with the fantasy of a tryst with the florist, when I deliberated her gold band and let its implications slide, it wasn't a love story that I was searching for. I only wanted to corral a transitory touch, seize a fugitive intimacy for a moment in time. I'm not looking for love. I'm not looking for a relationship. I've walked that tightrope and fallen.

Like halved hearts, the petals lay in my lap. If there was a way, if I could weave them together into perfect valentines, would I? I gathered the petals and watched as they fluttered, one by one, to the floor.

FREE-FALL

I've fallen into myself. As if I'd leapt from an airplane and floated like a sky diver to the ground, I've fallen, engulfed in the most pleasurable sensations...Where have I been these last few months — lost in an enchanted forest? A victim of a sorceress's spell? Like Dorothy, I've awakened to find myself home, once again.

A hard pit entombed in soft, delectable fruit. I am delicious and ripe and full. People are noticing. "You're different," they say. "You glow." They're right. I'm a star who's pushed through thick, black clouds.

Something unexpected has happened. My connection to *her* has dissipated. I rolled out of bed and the leg cuffs were gone. I'm free from the heaviness of what *she's* done.

A burst of light dances on the edge of the sky and I'm no longer afraid. I'm not that hollow reed that she used to play so easily with an invisible breath of air. I feel strong and empowered.

I've let go. My fear and devastation move through me. I have nothing left for *her* — *she* who blamed only me. *She* who looked me in the eye and lied. I don't care. I don't care about *her*. I don't care about *her* lies. They will leave *her* hopeless and solitary in a wintry tomb.

I have a vision of her, a prisoner to her own darkness, alone and spiritless. I'm through with the deceit. She may fool herself but she no longer tricks me. I have nothing left for her.

I've fallen into myself. Now, nothing can be taken away. Outside of me, things evaporate like rain in a New Orleans heat wave. I don't care. Inside, I'm the same person. My connection to myself is complete and full.

I have an impromptu lover. Through her, I explore myself. We're caring for a night, passionate for a night and the next morning when she walks out the door, I'm confident that a piece of my heart is not smuggled out under her jacket. When she goes, I'm left unscathed.

Simone desires me. Late at night, she slips into my bed like a sex-hungry boy. She's all over me —

always all over me. With her, I feel sexy. I feel alluring. How long since I've pulled on those thigh-high boots? Those silk gloves? That lacy camisole? This new lover inspires me. With her, I wear the lingerie that I tucked in my drawer so many months ago.

She steals her way between my sheets, between my legs, between my slippery folds of skin. Her fingers push into me. How hungry I am. How desperate she makes me. She sucks me, leaving purple welts on my flesh, bruises between my thighs.

I wait, wet for her. Dim lights. Soft music. She comes to me, always wanting more. Always pushed by desire. She lifts me — how strong she is! Carries me — how determined! Holds me as if she's all there ever was.

Long after she's left, I stand in front of the mirror and consider her marks all over my flesh.

I tumble over and over. I soar in lazy circles toward the earth. Far below, tiny figures run for cover. All of them scurry except for one who stands with arms outstretched. I am falling. Falling. I no longer need *her,* or her, or anyone. Falling. Falling down toward that figure whose arms open wide. Like a waterfall daredevil, I somersault toward myself.

Simone comes to me late at night. I dress in garters and lace for her. I wear shadows and darkness for her and she craves me even more.

Falling. Falling down I go.

She comes in my room and carries me to the bed.

On my belly for her, face in the pillows, I wait as she ties me with scarves to each bedpost. My arms are restrained. My legs are bound tight. She steals the pillow from me and brings me home to myself with a blindfold. Suddenly, blackness and solitude enfold me. We're in a deserted cave. I'm dependent on her to lead the way. Our breaths are simultaneous in slow, steady rhythm.

Each subtle sound alerts me. The scent of a lit match is strong. Perhaps she's burning incense? A candle? I keep my breath in time with hers.

With her, for a night, I'm malleable putty. Let her do what she wants, I'm a willow tree, dipping and swaying in a strong spring breeze. Each tomorrow, when she walks out the door, I'm visibly intact.

Falling. Falling down I go. Closer to the ground. I see everyone has scattered except for the silhouette of myself dancing in circles across a petal-laden field. Toward her I whirl. Toward her I descend.

On the bed, face down and bound, I wear nothing but a lace garter and thigh highs. What she asks for is exactly what she gets. The intensity of her breath deepens and I become lightheaded trying to match her exhalations.

Somewhere in the room, she watches me. Her sharp focus slices the tender flesh of my ass. I feel vulnerable and strong, all at once. Tied to the bed, I am hers for a moment, but as invincible as midnight. Is she standing at the foot of the bed? By my side? If I quiet my thoughts, I'll hear her fiery breath once again. I try to move but the scarves are tighter than I had thought — which is nice, which is so, so nice. I like the tension in my arms and legs. I like this sense of being on edge, of reveling in the possibility of letting go.

Perhaps it is a peacock feather that she's grazing across my back and over my ass. Soft and sensual, light and tentative. Letting go, but not. Falling. Falling. Down I go. No attachments. No demands. No one to be accountable to. I sail like the majestic hawk across a summer sky deep into sunset canyons. It's chilly and I hope for warmth.

My considerate lover doesn't disappoint me. The tickle is replaced by the surprise of melting wax. Down my back. Hot but good. Wet but good. An uncontrolled excitement ignites and my clitoris feels charged with electric current. She dribbles the heat between the cheeks of my ass. I squirm with delicious pleasure. This is so sweet. She is so sweet. She tells the truth with each move she makes. I know this, I can feel it in the hardening wax.

She bites my ass. Pinches my ass. Spills liquid heat down the crack of my ass. I love her for this. Love her, love her, love her for this. The feather, the wax, the feather, the wax.

She surrenders her busy hand to my pussy and offers two, then three, of her rough and ready fingers. She pulls my cheeks apart and dips one teasing finger between the cleft. Down into the soft, she burrows. She buries her fingers somewhere in the damp and slips, just one, along the rim of my ribbed slit. Her finger is a desperate yellow jacket and I'm a rose on the verge of a spectacular bloom.

Her finger flutters on the inner edge of my pussy.

Deeper.
Why can't I ask for what I want?
Deeper.
Why can't I just say it?
She lingers and I teeter precariously on purple pleasure. The tension is tight in my thighs. My wrists ache. I want her. I want her. If my hands were free, I'd grab hers, I'd force her teasing fingers deep, deep, deep.

She teases my cunt but then moves her finger toward my ass slit. Oh God, does she want her finger in my ass — my unshielded, naked ass? Tied down, no place to go . . .

Falling, falling into myself. It's dark and she's here, but not. By myself. By myself. If I stop her, nothing can be taken. Nothing nothing.

I can sense tears beneath the silky blindfold. Falling, falling. I will catch myself. I am down on the ground waiting, certain and clear with arms outstretched.

Then why am I crying?

Finger in my pussy. Thumb against my ass. She spills a trail of wax down my back.

Falling. Falling.

I spiral, nosedive, catapult — fast, quick, hard. Right into the palm of an open hand, I blast, splash, crash.

"No, please stop."

Morning. She blows me a kiss and walks out the

door. Last night her desire for trespass pushed a boundary. A dangerous place where I tumble into the palm of another's opened hand?

Not me.

Not like that.

I must be cautious of where I fall.

HOW I LIKE IT

"I can make you come. Just tell me how you like it," she whispers.

Her breath is hot. Heat sizzles in my ear then surges like a stream of electricity through me. I'm aroused to that place again — that unbearable, dangerous place. A constant throbbing radiates from between my legs and from deep in my sex. I totter on a sharpened edge. Another minute of this, another second of this and I may have to sink my teeth into the tender flesh of her arm to keep from crying out in delicious agony.

"Just tell me what you like." Her words cut the silence once again.

A paragraph or two away from absolute pleasure — if I string some words together, weave them into a line or two, then release will be mine. She promises me this. *Say what you want. Whisper it. Close your eyes and take a chance.* But I can't. I can't say it, no matter how hard the ache, how insistent the pressure is in my swollen clit. I just can't.

Except for the narrow flicker of light a single candle brings, the room is dark. A shadow dances erratically across the bedroom wall. Her lips are still pressed against my ear. "Tell me. Tell me." She kisses my cheek, my forehead, my eyes. "Please."

I consider what she's asking and do a quick scan of the room. The slender light from the candle is far too bright. If I reveal too much, there'd be no place to hide.

Her fingers linger on the fringe of my pussy then inch between the folds. She's been touching me for over an hour. Or has it been two? Three? She won't let me look at my watch — she says time doesn't matter. It does to me.

A fingertip flirts with the side of my clitoris. "Tell me."

I close my eyes and imagine the words. *Move your finger across the top in a light circle. Yes, like that. Like that. Now back to the side. Real, real slow. Follow the wedge of flesh down to the lips. Yes. Yes. Now go back up. Use more pressure. Now down. Now back.*

"Tell me, baby. Tell me." She swirls her finger

along the rim of my opening. "Do you want me inside or on your clit?"

"Everything you do is good," I whisper. I like that the candlelight is weakening. I feel safer, less vulnerable.

She shimmies one finger into the slit and hesitates. "In or not."

I arch my hips and thrust forward. Her finger pierces deeper into me.

"Oh, so you want me in." Her tone is low and sexy.

Yes. Yes. Yes, I want her in. *Go as deep as you can. Yeah. Yeah. Deep, deep, deep. Then pull out real, real slow. Oh good. Oh sweet. Now up to my clit. Draw my cream up and across my clit. Can you feel it? Am I hard? Erect?* God, I feel like I am. But I say nothing. Absolutely nothing.

I reach to my pussy. My clitoral flesh is thick and full — like a blackberry. Images of last weekend's trip to the river float to mind. We had hiked along the bank. Blackberries hung heavy and ripe on a scraggly bush. She plucked one and caressed my mouth with the sun-heated fruit.

"Feel it with your tongue."

The fruit was plush, fleshy, warm. I licked it and lapped it until she finally surrendered it to my mouth.

Like a single, fat blackberry, my clit is perched between her fingers. Pinch it. Just pinch it a bit. Like a berry. Squirt some stain on your fingers. Please. Please. Squeeze it like that. Like that. Like that.

Her finger is in me, but not moving. I know what she's planning. She'll hold it like that, maybe jerk it a time or two, until I can't stand it, and then she'll fuck me. I can almost come that way. Almost. I'll get so close and then a curtain comes crashing down. Flying on her fingers at one hundred rpm's, I'll suddenly remember forgotten dry cleaning, a dental appointment or an unmade call. I hate that.

She wiggles her finger against the walls of my pussy. I'm wet. I can feel slippery sex juice on my thighs. If she'd only take her other hand . . . if she'd only stretch my outer lips wide apart and then flick me with her tongue.

Remember the blackberries? Would you stretch my outer lips open, clamp me, hold me tight and then do me like we did those blackberries?

That hot day at the river we had pushed our way through wild flowers, honey-plump bees and blackberry bushes. The summer heat was intense. Sweat beaded above her upper lip. She picked a handful of berries. Some for me. Some for her. One at a time, that's how we ate them. The tip of her tongue swirled on each round, plush seed-sack. She sucked a berry into her mouth, pressed it with her tongue and dark purple squirted onto her lips. She kissed me and the juice stained my lips. She passed a crushed berry from her mouth to mine. Mashed warm and moist, it slid down my throat.

Would you do it like that? Your tongue on the seed-sack bead of my clit, little circles, light circles. Press me, flatten me, until I squirt stain all over your mouth? Squirt stain all over your chin? Come kiss me — bring my juice to my face. Come kiss me before it dries. Smear it on my face, your face, mine. Put your fingers back near my clit. Please? Please? Just on the side. Just on the edge. Like that. Yes.

Good. Like that. Yes. Sweet, sweet, sweetheart, like that.

The words push hard in my throat.

"Can you help me thaw?" I had asked the first time she came to my bed.

"You want to thaw?" She looked me square in the eyes. "That's my specialty — melting you as far as you'll go."

Help me thaw?

What had I been thinking?

She's come to melt me with her fiery power. She's come to liquefy me with her uncompromising demands. Her finger, still in my pussy, has barely moved. Her breath is hard in my ear. I grab her arm and push, jamming her fingers deeper. She knows what I want now.

"Got you, baby. Baby, baby, baby," she mutters. "I'll fuck you now."

She rams her fingers in and out. She can go so fast. She can go nonstop. The rhythm of her breathing accelerates, countering each thrust. And oh, oh, oh, she is so good. So good. So good. I get hot. I ride the edge of pleasure like a spinning gyroscope.

"Okay, yes. Okay, yes." I crush my mouth into her shoulder. My teeth seize her flesh. Almost. Almost.

"Keep ... fucking ... you ... like ... this?" Her words ride a torrent of quick breaths.

The blackberries had basked in the summer sun for hours. With a single kiss, hot, squishy blue-violet passed from her tongue to mine. Thick blackberries, pulpy blackberries — on my lips, my chin, my cheeks.

I feel so lush, so juicy. I am succulent blackberries warmed and ready. Run your fingertip back to my clitoris. Isn't it just like a fat, meaty sun-baked berry? Would you cradle it between your thumb and finger — maybe squeeze it? Maybe tug it? Maybe try to pluck it? Oh yes. I like when you use a bit of pressure. I like when you compress, squash, crush that spongy bit of sex fruit.

Oh and my nipples! Can you see how they've raised into firm, tight points. Could you . . . would you capture one between your teeth? Yes. Bite down. Easy though. Easy, easy, easy. Keep milking my clit. Keep working my clit. Yes. Please. Please.

Almost. Almost. Her hand is sopping wet. Each time she slams into me a slapping sound fills the room. Wet hand. Wet pussy. My clit feels tripled in size. I nudge it back and forth with my thumb. I pinch it between my fingers.

Those blackberries. Those, those blackberries. Supple, like my clit. Puffy, like my clit. Ruffled, swollen, voluptuous, like my clit. Back and forth I knead the flesh. Buttery damp coats my fingers, soaks my fingers. She's still fucking me. She's still ramming me with all she's got. Wetter and wetter. Almost. Almost. As if liquid rubber has filled each wrinkled pleat, my clit suddenly stiffens. I'm riding it now. I'm cruising it now.

"More, baby? More, baby?" Fast, hard words hurtle from her mouth and sting my neck. She's sucking me, biting me. "Go, baby. Go, baby."

Almost. Almost. If she'd pinch my nipple, if she'd push my fingers out of the way and churn my clit herself. And then, real fast, if she'd —

Shit, did I turn off the oven?

A black curtain slams between us. Her arm stops thrusting. Her lips stop sucking.

"Where did you just go?" Her voice is tough.

I'm quiet. I hate this part.

"Where did you just go?" she says again.

"Kitchen?" Somehow the word spills out as a question.

"Kitchen, huh." She sits up. "Kitchen, huh."

"Did I turn off the oven?" I feel like a fool.

"Yes," she whispers. She positions herself between my legs. "The oven is off." She lies on top of me. She turns my head to the side. "No one moves until you tell me how you like it."

"I like everything you do." My eyes are closed. It's safer that way.

"Nope. Not moving." Her entire body weight pins me to the bed.

"But I do —"

"Nope." She grabs my wrists and pulls my arms above my head. "Nope, nope, nope."

I clench my eyes tight. Her body feels so strong, so forceful, so in control. Her breasts push into mine. She is covered with sweat. The slippery, hot damp is earthy, is animal, is sex stripped raw. Her ankles press mine and with a fast push, she separates my legs even farther. Pressure restrains my arms, tension secures in my legs. My clit pounds in delicious misery. *Tell her. Tell her. Tell her.*

Butterflies skitter in my belly. Tell her? Could I go into the other room and write it down for her and send it in the mail? Fax it? Could I go to a pay phone and give her a call?

"Tell me, now." She is uncompromising. Her hands clutch my wrists.

If only I had a blindfold on. If only the room were pitch-black.

I open my eyes the tiniest bit. The room is darker. The candle flame leaps on the last of the wick. Do words disappear when spoken in the dark? Could I pass them through some sort of filter? Could I be certain of what I'd say . . .

"But I got to tell you," she had said that first time. "I'm coming from the place of keeping things easy, keeping things safe. No involvement beyond right here in bed. Agree?"

"No involvement," I replied. "Exactly what I want."

"Believe me, it's best this way."

I had nodded and then watched in anticipation as she had unzipped her pants . . .

Careful. One word. One word only.

"Blackberry." My whisper seems to reverberate in the room.

"Blackberry?" On a heated breath, her reply hisses through my ear, burns a red-hot trail to my nipples, singes my clit and settles deep in my womb. Ongoing, the fire expands each time she exhales.

On that river bank, she had perched a single blackberry on her fingertips and held it only inches from my mouth. "See this?" she said seductively. She slowly worked the chubby clump of fruit. Within seconds, the inky juice had dribbled onto her finger.

My clit throbs as that image projects itself across my mind. *Prop it on your fingers like that. Twist it gently. Wring it carefully. Circle my slit at the same time.*

"Like you did the blackberry —" I mutter, closing my eyes again. God, this is so, so difficult. I can dress in lace and thigh-highs, I can tempt and tease, but if I start talking — how will I control the words?

How will I keep the shield raised? Will I cross that line from how I want her to touch me to how much more I may need?

She is quiet. She is still. Is she thinking? Will she get out of bed? Walk out the door? Have I already revealed too much?

"Those blackberries were so sweet," she says softly. She slides her hand from my wrist, down my arm, to caress my cheek. Her lips are tender on mine. To my breasts, to my belly, her hand floats like an autumn leaf. "Remember how they felt? How thick? How plump?" Her words are muffled as she kisses my neck. Her fingers weave through my sex hair then slip between the folds.

"Yes. Yes, I remember."

She captures my clit and squeezes it lightly. "Then tell me."

Her fingers compress then release. Compress then release. My clit is harder than it's ever been. Oh God, oh God, oh God. All I want now, all I need now, if she'd just —

She doesn't stop. I imagine her fingers on that chunky bit of fruit. She'd manipulate it. She'd pump it. She'd drain it. There is so much I want, so much I crave. If only those words — stuck in the back of my throat, lodged there — if only I could push those electric words out.

The flame folds into itself and the room falls into complete dark. Her fingers feel so sweet on my flesh. Desire snakes through me. Now. Now. Now. Now is the only moment. If she'd only —

"Twist it," I mutter.

I bury my face into her shoulder. If I could disappear, slither out the room with that last bit of light, get in my car and just keep driving, I would. Her fingers grasp my clit even tighter. And yes, oh yes, she's got me now.

I bite her shoulder. *Juice it like that blackberry. Make it purple. Make it spurt.*

"More, baby? Huh, baby?"

"Don't stop. Yes, there. More. More. More." Wild and uninhibited pleas pour from me, stream from me, cream from me. I'm hot. Close. Out of my body. Over my body. Racing around the room.

Now circle my slit. Now strum my clit. Again and again. Easy. Easy. Yeah. Yeah. Was that me begging?

She moves her finger across my entrance and to my clit. Across my entrance and to my clit. Almost. Almost. The oven is off. The doors are locked. The car lights extinguished. The iron unplugged. Oh yes. Oh yes. Oh yes. Oh yes. This. This. This. This. This is how I like it.

Dear God, am I still intact?

SURRENDER

The sun is warm. The sky is dusty blue. The hill is steep and I'm out of breath before the cabins disappear behind the trees. Not too far along the road, we veer onto a path that curves up and around the hill. She leads, I follow.

"You know what to do if we see a bear?"

I hate when women ask me questions like that. Yes. Of course I know what to do — the *real* question is whether I, or anyone in their right mind, would actually hang around long enough to do it. My favorite, most ridiculous rule of thumb? *If you come upon a bear, don't run.* Yeah, right.

"Sure." I try to sound as dependable as the next good-time gal, but bottom line, we see a bear, I'm outta here.

We climb on. The farther we walk, the more I struggle with the bear thing. She can follow all the rules — stand firm, make eye contact, act large, slowly back away (after all, she *is* the butch). Meanwhile, I'll race like hell for help. Makes sense to me. I scan the thickness of the trees that surround the road. Was there a bear lurking behind every trunk?

On she hikes until we reach a flat plateau where she turns and kisses me. Caught in her embrace, I'm still able to do a discreet survey of the nearby forest. No bears in sight.

On this ridge, the heat is intensified. The breeze is light but noticeable. Like her touch — like her touch as she lifts off my T-shirt and unhooks my bra. She says I'm so much a woman. She says my hair is gorgeous. She unzips my jeans and pulls down my pants.

She uses my shirt and jacket as a makeshift bed and leads me to the ground. The sun canopies us in a bright haze. The breeze grazes my skin like a satin sheet. I close my eyes and savor how alert my senses are. The sun speaks to my belly, my face, my breasts.

I steal a glance at the surrounding area. No bears.

She pulls my legs apart and stretches open the

lips of my pussy. The breeze kisses my pampered flesh. The sun laps the skin. I close my eyes and bask in the luxury of nature's caress.

She holds me open. "You should see how beautiful you are in the sunlight. This is the first time I've had a chance to really look at you. To really see everything." She stretches the outer lips even farther.

The idea of her scrutinizing my nakedness leaves me vulnerable and exposed yet this very self-consciousness arouses me. I close my eyes. It's easier for me if I hide in the dark.

She runs her fingertips along the inside of my thighs. "You are beautiful," she says. "You have an extraordinary pussy."

I wonder about *extraordinary*. I've sat with a hand mirror and stared at my sex. If I were the lover would I be pleased? *A pussy made for fucking,* one lover had said. *A voluptuous pussy. A luscious pussy.*

She flutters her fingers. Her touch strikes deep. Everything she does feels perfect. Even so, it's still difficult to simply surrender to the sensations. With her, I want to try. She touches me right to the core of my sex.

The sun is hot. Beads of sweat pool above my lips and at the nape of my neck. I lick my lips and taste a trace of salt.

"Can you feel this?" she asks. "There's a little rod under the skin. All the way from here —" Her fingers have captured my clitoris and are lightly squeezing along the length of it. "— to here."

The sensation is incredible. I don't want her to

stop. "A rod?" I ask, as if, perhaps, I could tempt her to continue kneading and examining the tiny shaft.

"You're getting redder," she whispers. "Redder and bigger. You must be engorging with blood." She spreads the lips even farther apart. Like a thick, warm tongue, the sun beats down on the exposed flesh while her fingers tease, pull, tug, jerk the rod.

I glance for bears. There's nothing in sight. The ground is hard beneath me. Sticks and rocks dig into my back. The breeze sings through the trees and for a moment, I watch them sway.

She's all over my sex. She's pressing me and moving — she can pulse her hand nonstop. Once, she masturbated in front of me. I was amazed how fast she could drive her fingers. Now, as we lie on a plateau somewhere in the woods, she's working me.

I know, if I'd just surrender, she'd take me there. But surrender is never that easy. Not one hundred percent surrender. I wish it were. If I could snap my fingers and fall into immediate release from myself, I'd be so pleased. And her fingers are flying back and forth on my clit and she's talking about how rigid it is, how thick, how blood-flushed.

I'm mercury slowly moving up a glass thermometer. I'm a pot of water on the verge of boil. Surrender. *I know I can.*

"What about this —" She stops.

I open my eyes and shield the sun with my hand.

"What if I held you apart —" She waves a blunted twig in front of my face. "— with this."

She hinges my bulky, outer lips with the tiny stick.

Ouch! It hurts momentarily but the idea of it has me so stirred that I decide to move past the discomfort. She's smiling. She laughs. It's obvious that her plan pleases her. She shimmies a shorter twig between the lower, smaller lips. *Ouch!*

She is so clever. Her sweet imagination intertwines with a nasty streak that delights me. New ideas, clever ideas — like using the twigs to hold me open — the sort of things that I fabricate for the stories I write. I like that. I like that a lot.

I try to lean forward so I can see those sticks, but I can't. They prick the flesh when I move. So I stay back, do one last scan for bears and finally decide to relax, to do my best to simply let go.

She pushes her face into my pussy and licks all the places she can around those thin sticks. It's a delicious torture. A delicious, delicious torture. It's like this for a few minutes until she plucks the sticks and starts strumming her fingertips across my clit.

Her fingers flip faster and faster. A gorgeous fever races through me. She falls into me — fingering my clit, rubbing my folds, patting my pussy again and again. I'm riding a wave. I'm balanced on a surf board and cruising.

High above this plateau, I'm perched on the edge of a cliff. I peer down at us — two minute figures in the dust. We're surrounded by a blazing circle that seems to radiate from her hand. Her focus is intent and she seems to pull the sun rays into a single beam that bursts into a protective ring of fire.

"You are so beautiful." Her words are muffled by the rhythm of her hand.

If she'd keep watch, then maybe I could surrender?

Her fingers are a thousand tongues lapping at my clit. Her hand is powerful. Her palm covers my slippery clitoris and in fast, hard pushes, she whips back and forth. Again and again, she goes on and on. The sun blazes. The breeze is on the upswing.

An eagle soars in the distance. I'm tempted to leap from this precipice and follow behind. I'd see through the trees, down to the place where the bears find their prey. Then maybe I'd feel safe?

"Don't run," she whispers.

If she'd keep watch, then maybe . . . ?

Her fingers are quivering cobras — biting, nipping, striking my erect shaft.

And if I open my eyes and a hundred bears encircle us?

"Don't run," she mutters again and again.

I clench my eyes tighter. My body aches for hard release. Somewhere high above, I balance on the edge of the cliff. Surrender is no longer easy. Not for me. Not one hundred percent. And if there are bears? And cougars? And things to fear? If I let go for her — will I recover? Will I ever recover?

I've been mauled. I've closed my eyes one time too many. Act large? Don't run? How many times have I fallen prey to predatory heartbreakers? No eye contact. No acting large — I run like hell when it gets too close.

Her fingers skate across my clit and a thunderstorm builds beneath the flesh. She keeps going for more and more. Each time she takes me, she tries to break some kind of boundary. Like in my ass. Like with her fist. Like spanking me when I start to get hot.

She hooks her fingers deep inside my slit and starts her search. There's a spot she's found, somewhere inside of me, that she can work in a way to make me ejaculate. She presses it or pushes it or whatever she does and a deep burning escalates until I squirt. She thinks that's so hot and always gets a cocky attitude after I've come that way.

"I wish you could see this. I wish you could be down here at my side and see how you look in this sun."

I feel a familiar pressure deep inside and know she's found the place. I'm working with her but fighting against her all the same. A crazy paradox — wanting her to have me but resisting on a level that I just can't name. Isn't she frightened of bears? Would she really stand firm and look one in the eyes?

"Oh, baby. I got you now." That cocky edge is in her voice.

She's got me now. That heated burn is coming on strong. Any moment, out of control, a tidal wave of who I am could spill on her hands.

A noise somewhere breaks the climb. A bear? A Goddamn bear out there? I consider racing as fast as I can down the hill and out of sight. Or? Or?

Her fingers stroke. Her fingers stir. *She's got me now. She's got me now.*

If she'd keep watch . . . if she'd keep watch . . .

"Don't run, baby. Don't run, sugar."

She's loving me now. She's on that spot and it feels so sweet and nothing could stop me now. I'm invincible. I'm unstoppable. She's on it now and I feel so good, so good that . . . that . . .

"Yeah, yeah, yeah." She's talking from a million miles away.

. . . so good that I don't care about shit. I don't care about anything but sweet release. Surrender, surrender, okay fine, surrender — and if there are bears, well then let them come.

THE SHOOTING STAR

Last night she came over. Last night she came into my room and then — almost against my will? my better judgment — she went even further. Deep. She said for me to get on my knees — *oh no, oh no* — but I did. On my knees for her, I bent over. She got behind me and grabbed my ass — *oh no, oh no.*

She was slippery from sweat. Sliding her belly against my ass, her breasts on my back — she grabbed my ass, grabbed my ass and pulled my cheeks apart. She stopped. Just held me like that. I was face down. My eyes were closed. I felt her taking in every secret part of me — parts I never expose to anyone — *oh no.*

She kept me spread and I felt her take me in, devour me with her eyes. If I could have buried my face into the mattress, if I could have somehow disappeared, I would have. Exposed. Exposed. Her hands pulled my ass apart. She molded me like slippery clay. Like oiled bread dough, she kneaded me.

I was pliable. I was flexible. I was opened and closed all at once. She plunged her fingers into the puckered slit of my ass. If I could have, I would have torn into the mattress with my teeth, burrowed far into a cave. I wanted to escape from her direct vision, from her even more direct touch.

Face buried in the bedding, ass high in the air, I made myself available to her. I was a reluctant, greedy beggar — insisting no, pleading yes.

She didn't stop, would not stop — in my cunt, in my ass — as deep as she could go. She was all over me. I was all over her. My sweat, my cum, my secret oils, my scents — I wanted to run forever, hide and not be seen. Seen, seen, like never before — she was behind me, spreading my ass and seeing it all. I was desperate to escape. Desperate to succumb. I wanted her to reach as deep as she could, to grab me, to pull me inside out, upside down. Ass high. Open but tight, ready but not.

She kissed me. Kissed me and opened me wider. Her tongue skimmed the most private place. There was no place to escape. *Oh no.*

"No," I said. "No." I squirmed. The foam pillow captured my words.

Lost, fading, evaporating into naked pleasure — I

was vulnerable to her. Tears raced from my eyes, down my cheeks. Too vulnerable. I loved her in that moment. In that moment I was hers. Hers. Hers. Hers. Her tongue — a warm, moist spear — pierced into me.

No, but yes. Stop, but go. Over a waterfall, I tumbled. I somersaulted in thick, heated air. I was balanced on her tongue. She had come into me and I was nothing but her.

Naked. Vulnerable. Scared. Young. *Would she love me now? Take care of me? Wrap me in her warmth and whisper tenderness? Would she? Shooting across midnight on a lightning hot tongue. She and I.*

"Why are you doing this," I cried. I screamed. I was lost in the wonder of primitive pleasure. I was blind and her tongue was my sight.

I wanted to cry a million tears for all the love lost, to be carried away on a wave of sadness. A stream of salty tears streaked my face. Sweat pooled on my belly. Her fingers dipped into the damp. I rode across an ocean on her hand.

On her mouth, I rode a hurricane. On her mouth, I slid down the arc of the rainbow to a treasure of jewels. Rubies, diamonds and gold awaited me. On her fluttering fingertips, I was an extension, a projection. Into an illusion, I spiraled.

Oh no.

Does she know she plays with fire? Is she aware that her touch lights the sky with dazzling fireworks?

Behind closed-tight eyes, I watched the darkness slip away. Open to her, vulnerable to her, a layer of who I am peeled from me like snake skin.

BABY WANTS MORE

"Do you have to leave?" I blurted, immediately regretting my words and their implications. She stopped at the door and turned. "I just thought perhaps . . ."

Perhaps what?

She glanced at her watch and smiled her bad-boy smile. "My baby want some more?"

I stood there but said nothing. After all, what was there to say — that I was wavering? That the boundaries we had so clearly set seemed too harsh? No emotional involvement, she had said, and I had, all too gladly, agreed.

"My baby need more?" She sauntered toward me — keys in one hand, leather jacket in the other.

Yes. Her baby wanted more. More. More. More. But what I wanted more of wasn't what she had in mind — was it?

She had pressed me to go further.

To give way to her.

To surrender . . .

Dangling from a parachute, I coast with the wind.

Don't ask about me, I don't want to tell.

Don't tell me about you, I don't want to know.

Emotionally uninvolved. As she was and where I should stay. After all, I have no illusions about romance. Isn't that what I've been saying?

"I just thought perhaps . . ." I averted my focus from her firecracker eyes to the thick silver buckle on her bike boot. "What I mean . . . What I was wondering . . ."

"Yes, baby?" She was inches from me. Her cologne swept me into a haze of desire.

"Do you have to leave? I mean, *always?* "

She backed up slightly. "Meaning?"

"Sometimes . . . maybe . . . just sometimes, though . . . I wish you'd want more."

"Baby, I always want more," she muttered.

"I mean, more than what it is." I kept staring at the floor.

She shifted her stance. "Baby, like we agreed. What we have is the 'more.' "

Yes. Of course — what we have is the more.

I looked her straight in the eyes, offered her a flirtatious smile then headed for the bedroom.

As I walked, I untied my robe and let it slip, slowly, to the floor.

"Yes," I said, resigned. "Your baby wants more."

THE UNGUARDED
MOMENT

THE UNGUARDED MOMENT

A wire is stretched tightly between where I stand and somewhere far in the horizon. Uncertainty looms like a gray cloud. What's out there beyond? I spin between the desire to walk the wire and the urge to stay safe. I want more, but don't. I ask for more, yet watch my words slip to the floor like a silk robe.

One foot moves cautiously in front of the other. Slow. Slow. Slow. One step and I stop. Another and I stop. Balanced, I'm a ballerina on a pinpoint. Even so, I wobble.

* * * * *

"Do you mind sitting next to a stranger?" She was dressed in black. Her suit — Armani? Lauren? — was most probably a man's, tailored for her slim, sleek build. Short, streaked-blond hair was swept back from her face. All seats were occupied around the large circular banquet table except the one next to me. The awards dinner was about to begin. I edged the vacant chair back slightly.

"You here alone?" She settled in next to me.

"Sort of." I knew everyone at the table but bottom line, I was without a date.

"Me too." She sipped from the water glass. "It would be nice to have someone to chat with. I'm probably the only woman here from Washington."

I concentrated on her eyes. An odd familiarity struck me — hadn't I seen eyes like that somewhere before?

In most instances, strangers are my favorite companions. They are mirrors. Who I know myself to be reflects from them and returns to me wrapped in a warm cocoon. I can say whatever I want and not be touched. Dinner. Dessert. I can be anything and then go home completely intact.

Unless, of course . . .

a stranger has eyes like those.

Eyes that are filled with a thousand diamond phrases.

All I could think of,
the only recourse I had
was to reach for my pen and write.

116

Something about this stranger called forth an image of the stack of glittery words, now bound and imprisoned, on my bedroom closet shelf. A sudden urge to tell her the seat was taken, I was here with a lover — anything, to force her to leave — burned through me like cheap whiskey.

"You okay?" She looked at me intently.

No problem. Not really. Hadn't I spent these last few months rescuing myself? "For a moment, you reminded me of someone, that's all."

"Bad, huh?"

"Just a memory, nothing more," I replied. Sometimes the desire to fall to pieces overwhelmed me.

"Tell me about it," she said as though my reminiscences could somehow matter.

Maybe after dinner we'd walk to the terrace. Maybe she'd take me in her arms. Could I have the luxury of an unguarded moment? Could I have a temporary respite, a break in the arduous task of self-defense?

I felt myself float toward the crystal chandelier. "Let's just say I'm jaded," was all I said.

"About romance? About love?"

I shrugged.

"Love and romance, huh," she replied as if I had answered.

"I've got nothing left," I offered.

"Nothing left to give?" The focus of her eyes on me was direct.

Attempting to break her incessant attention, I glanced slowly around the table.

"Meaning?" she persisted.

"Doesn't matter," I conceded. "What I want . . . this thing . . . doesn't exist. I can't put it into words —"

She stared right through me. "Sure you can."

Sure I could—*unless a stranger has eyes like hers.* I was quiet.

"Sure you can," she said again.

I shook my head.

"Just say the first word you think of." She was relentless.

The first word? I peered at the ice in my water glass and imagined myself melting. The first word. "Surrender," I said. A breath and a word, nothing more.

"Surrender to . . . ?"

"I don't know —" I felt a vague uneasiness. "Just surrender."

She leaned in close. "I could take you there."

I shot her a hard glance. Who the hell was this woman?

"Not possible." My tone was dismissive.

"You underestimate me." She tapped the bowl of her spoon with her finger all the while she stared at me.

Those eyes — in a moment, I could fall into the promises they held.

Those eyes — in a second I could spill all of my emptiness in a single breath.

"Washington is a thousand miles from here," I managed.

"You underestimate me," she said again. "A two-hour plane ride and . . ." She snapped her fingers. ". . . we're having dinner. And when I'm not there in person, one telephone call and I've transported myself to your room." It was quiet for a moment and then she continued. The intensity of her voice drew me in. "I'm a sorceress. At night, I'll saddle clouds and fly to you on the midnight-winds." As if lost in thought, she said nothing and then suddenly, "If I sent you a ticket, would you meet me somewhere for a weekend? Would you give me a chance?"

Give her a chance?

The chandelier hung overhead like an elaborate rhinestone brooch. I wondered what would happen if I simply closed my eyes.

ACE OF HEARTS

You, sweet-talking girl, sent me a ticket. Before I could say *no thanks,* flee down the street and around the bend, I'm onboard a dream and flying to you. Like I'm perched on the wing of a seven-thirty-seven, cold pushes me but I hang on. Far below, snow-capped peaks and hard-edged mountains loom.

How did I get here? One moment I was writing in my diary about broken hearts, the next I'm cruising on the wing of a fast-paced jet. You sent me a ticket and I think, well, why not? A complimentary trip to the Oregon coast. I scribble promises in my journal. A two-day hiatus by the sea. A tryst with a reckless romantic and nothing more . . .

You sent me four dozen roses this week, a luxurious silk robe and seven hearts filled with exotic bath oils.

I have no illusions about romance. At a seaside haven, I'll stay in the moment but out of reach. I'm a gambler, a rambler — with nothing to fear. I can't be touched. Whatever valuables I had have already been stolen — no insurance and no return.

Don't ask about me. I don't want to tell. Don't tell me about you. I don't want to know.

But who did you love before you tempted me? Does she still wear your ring on an empty hand? Does she still have her heart on a tear-stained sleeve? Why have you come here, flirting with me? You're not the first girl to ask me how I want it. You're not the first to flash me your charms.

Round trip, please. Just drop me off where you found me. With a bankrupt heart I can only afford a day or two.

Today, without reason, I pulled that once-glittery stack of letters from the top of the closet, put them in the sink and saturated them with a stream of Clorox. Like the love-thief who sent them, the ink simply disappeared into hard-to-read lines.

I was thinking about that ticket and your run-away dreams — the flicker of hope, the hint of possibilities. The jack of hearts is tucked up your sleeve. The queen and king ride your breast pocket. And in your palm?

It may be a bluff. I remember the fast-talking hustler who dealt the last game. Her bleached-white letters fill my basin.

"Ante up," she had said. "Put it all in the pot."

There's nothing to lose when it's all been robbed, is there? Is there?

You toss twenty dollars into the pot.

"Lookin' good," you say like you're one heart from a royal flush.

I peek at my cards and contain my smile. Ace of hearts.

"I see your twenty and raise you ten."

RIVERBED

The restaurant overlooks the Pacific. The window by our table is directly above the sea. As though we're perched on the brink of the world, I peer into the dark. Far in the distance, a beam of light flickers. The light piercing the black night mesmerizes. I envision myself walking that ray to the place where the sky and the sea merge to a sharp edge.

"Where'd you just go?" Her voice pulls me back to the table.

"I was imagining walking across that beam." I point to the intermittent light.

She glances out the window. "That's the lighthouse we passed this afternoon."

I nod.

"Walk that, huh," she says. Her focus shifts to me. "Is it the light itself or the journey through darkness that appeals to you?"

Not one to chitchat; her questions are direct. Like this afternoon — when we strolled down the beach. The wind overpowered our words, limiting conversation to rock-sheltered alcoves. When she did speak, she mostly asked questions. Why did I say this? What did I mean by that? Her queries pushed me.

"I don't know," I had said. "I'm not sure." I shrugged.

"Think then. What exactly do you mean?"

I now stare at the illuminated path that penetrates the dark. *Is it the light itself or the journey through darkness that appeals to you?* Well? Which is it?

"I don't know," I reply, knowing all too well that this discussion won't end here.

"Sure you do." She's determined.

I'm quiet. She's going to sit there and look at me until I give her what she wants.

"I suppose it's the act — walking to the brink and touching the dark." I'm thinking hard, but not. This happens with her. Words come from nowhere yet somewhere, deep inside.

"And?" she presses. "What's out there in the dark?"

I look back to the light and consider her question.

Always asking — she reveals little about herself yet demands more and more from me. So? Who cares? A weekend on the Oregon coast. A fast tango in the arms of a dancer who then flies a thousand miles away. She's a stranger who's offered a glimpse in the mirror.

In most instances, strangers are my favorite companions. Who I know myself to be reflects from them and returns to me wrapped in a warm cocoon. I can say whatever I want and not be touched. Dinner. Dessert. I can be anything and then go home completely intact.

The beam blinks in the night. As I sit across from her, well aware of her eyes on me, a familiar hunger gnaws within me.

"What's out there in the dark?" she says again.

I glance at her momentarily and, in an effort to avoid her gaze, I return my attention to the light. *Simply let words come.*

The sporadic light beckons. I'm moving slowly across the glimmer to the place where it marries the dark.

"It's as though I'm staring into a black abyss," I say without thinking. "There's a hunger . . . a crazy hunger . . . that hounds me —"

I feel as though I'm hypnotized. As I speak, I'm floating down a well. Like Alice's descent to Wonderland.

"From the depths of the abyss, I hear voices. They scream and I can barely think. Somewhere at the bottom there's a place —" The image of a dry, cracked riverbed comes to me. "It's a riverbed where fast-rushing water once cut across the parched earth." I close my eyes and see lush plants bordering the river's bank. "It was once so green. So lush. I'm at the edge of this abyss and I consider diving — even though I know I'll slam hard into a barren dry riverbed."

I feel tears balanced on my lashes. Will I stumble into a cascade of tears? I peek at her. She's staring intently at me.

I break into a whisper, "I mourn so deeply the loss of the water, the loss of the green."

For some inexplicable reason, I feel naked. Vulnerable. I fiddle with my spoon. I run my finger on the rim of my glass. If I could, I would excuse myself, hurry to the restroom — but unleashing this image leaves me unable to move.

"The water. The green. Where has that gone?" she asks.

I drift back to the light. "It was stolen," I murmur. Were there any more words from that place where the light disappeared?

Nothing.

"Where has that gone?" She is urging me to step further along the beam.

I feel myself evaporating into light particles. And then, from sparkling flakes of electricity, the words continue. "I stood by, idle, while lovers smuggled every last bit of green, every last drop of blue. I slept with the enemy. Night after night, they kissed me and made love to me and all the while, they were stripping all there was from the riverbank. I didn't know I was being robbed." I fall into momentary silence. "I didn't know I was being robbed," I say again, shaking my head. An acute grief overwhelms me. "I led my lovers to the river and shared the plush, fertile beauty. I turned away for a moment —

or was it a night? a week? — and then turned back. Another plant was gone. The water was disappearing."

She lays her hand on mine. I struggle between pulling my hand from hers and grasping it tightly.

"I didn't care? Didn't understand?" I am floating in the light. "I brought them to this oasis. And then, one day I realized the extent of the devastation." I shift my focus from the ray of light and watch her fingertip rim the border of her spoon in smooth arcs. "Apparently, I've slit my own wrist."

I stare at my plate. I feel suddenly vacant. The urge to cry rushes through me like a flash flood. *Could I go now, please? Get in the car and drive away from the vision I've painted?*

"I've got something for you." She tucks cash under the bill and leads me from my seat.

She ushers me from the dining room, through the foyer and finally to a candlelit room. A sleek, black piano and bench are centered in the otherwise empty space. Her hand slips from mine and she crosses to the piano. Uncertain what to expect, I stand in the doorway.

She sits at the piano.

"I wrote this about you," she says without looking up. And with that, she begins to play.

An aubade? The music swirls and I drift into a dream — Two lovers part as the dawn breaks. The memory of evening's passion intertwines with the sorrow of the sunrise farewell. A gentle morning breeze awakens the poetry of lace curtains swaying, wind chimes dancing, a butterfly coasting. She's at the piano and I'm in a vision.

127

The mood of the music changes and the sun fades behind swift-falling dusk. She's brought to me sunset on a fall day. The notes lift and intertwine like twirling autumn leaves — a beautiful descent that is the harbinger of a dying season. Music born from someone who is no stranger to the wilting of love. An underlying resignation to sadness and loneliness weaves through the piece. Hauntingly familiar, the mournful music spirals through me until it settles deep in my soul. Suddenly, I'm immobilized in icy winter. A flurry of devastation swirls around me. A dirge to accompany the passing of hope. A single tear freezes on my cheek.

And then, as if she waves a wand and winter disappears — an unexpected shift warms into a lilting melody. Spring unveils and the urge to dance across the hilltop overwhelms me. The meadow blooms in a bouquet of orange and blue. Spinning in lazy circles, the butterflies and I . . .

The room falls into silence.

"I can take you there," she says. "Across that light, through the dark, right there. To the riverbed. Are you willing?" She walks to me and takes my hand. "It means not being safe. It means walking the edge and diving."

There is nothing I can say.

"I won't fall in love with you. I could disappear in a moment. It's all part of the plunge. Do you understand?"

I do, but I don't. Doesn't matter, I nod anyway. Yes. Ready for this. Hungry for this. Desperate for this.

She puts her arm around me and escorts me from the restaurant to the car. We drive in the dark along the windy roads of the Oregon coast. There's a light drizzle. The only sound is the swish of the wipers.

I feel hypnotized. I stare at quick-passing trees and somewhere between, I see us . . .

She takes my hand. Her flesh is winter-cold yet simmering with passion. Her fingers grasp my wrist and I know that I'm shackled and there's no way out.

She takes me to the edge of the light. She makes me look out from there where it's dark, desolate. She's right behind me, holding me, and yet, in that same moment she sits at the piano and begins to play.

"I wrote this about you."

Her music leaps from the piano like a whirlwind of flower petals. The abyss is suddenly showered in a colorful storm of flowers and music. Like tiny fireworks, each note lights the dark sky. Reds and yellows and greens sprinkle down toward the riverbed.

She is not behind me yet her breath is on my neck. Her fingers clamp my bleeding wrist and I watch in awe as those prism-petals light the sky in swirls. All the way down — like shooting stars from the blackness above the cliff — all the way down to the riverbed, they twirl.

And soon — or is it a long time? I can't be sure, but it seems like a minute, seems like an eternity — those raindrop-petals splash into the cracked bed. Colors ricochet from each blow and land on the bank of the river. Greens, yellows, reds, pinks. We're on the edge of the abyss. Her breath is heated music in my ear.

She says she won't love me, but she does. She says she could be gone in a moment but she won't. She flies like a hawk from where she stands and disappears to — oh God — to forever, but, but, the

129

riverbank is her. Is me. Water rushes and it's her.
Flowers bloom and it's me. The music goes on and
on and on and she's here . . .

The trees race past me.
I don't care what she says about *safe*. I don't care
about the edge. Her music springs forth long-awaited
possibilities.

The riverbed comes back to life
because she has brought this to me.
Oh, sweet God, I am so, so hungry.

TELEPHONE LOVERS

You whisper your desire from a thousand miles away and that easily, you have caressed me. I close my eyes and feel you. You touch me. Riding across the sky on a midnight wind, you come to me. In a second, in a solitary breath, you are in my room. I unbutton my pajamas for you. I open my legs for you. You touch me and a million stars spill from me to your hands. Tiny glittering lights flash on your fingertips. Sparks fly.

My nipples are red rubies. You reach to steal the precious gems from my breasts and slip them in your pockets. I know you. I know how you take what you want. I don't care. Every treasure that I have, I give freely.

A galaxy of stars whirls around my room. Dizzy, I hold onto you, grab onto you, fly with you as you race through the midnight and into the light of another universe. To another world, I ride your whispered words.

Desperate to retrieve each tender word as it flutters from your mouth like autumn leaves, I crawl on my knees. Tinted in September hues, your words lead me from summer into cold, into ice and then, with a simple whisper, I am springtime and each word spoken is another blossom — tender, soft, opening my heart.

"I am there with you," you say and I bask in torrid summer heat.

I climb on your back. I dig my fingernails into your flesh. I bite into your neck. I am crying. I am sobbing. I am hungry for so much more. The fields of a thousand flowers burst into bloom because —

Because you've come to me, across a midnight sky, bringing springtime and summer and autumn and snow. I dive into ice water, naked and alone, and glide through the darkness, slide through the darkness, ride through the darkness . . . coming . . .

coming . . . home.

You come to me across a midnight sky to touch
    me
touch me
love me until I cry.

THE TAIL OF THE SERPENT

THE HUNGER

"Tell me about the hunger." Her voice is steady, but I am certain of the reckless undertones.

It's eleven forty-five. I close my eyes and breathe easy. She's asking about the hunger again. She does this every time she calls.

From eleven o'clock on, I waited for the telephone to ring. Anticipating her return into my midnight life, I lit candles. I burned incense. Now in bed, I fall into the luxury of her voice. The candles flicker. A sultry, fragrant scent still hangs in the air.

"Tell me about the hunger." She is patient, but not.

She wants me to unravel the mystery for her, solve the deep longing that pushes me. I'm uncertain what to say. That thing, that craving, comes from a place where there aren't any words. Ancient. It has haunted me forever. I have journeyed deep into myself to find the dark goddess who drives me and demand answers. *Tell me about the hunger.* Sometimes desperate, sometimes despondent, sometimes exhilarated, I've trekked hazardous trails to track it down.

"I don't know, there aren't any words to explain." I lie alone in the room, alone in the house, alone in the world, wishing there were.

"Let's play a game," she says carefully.

I know about her games. She has ploys, she has plans — the fastest route down to the dark goddess is what she wants. And then what? What will she have when she sees me meet my match?

Doesn't matter. Nothing matters anymore. I've learned not to hold onto expectations — not about romance, not about love.

She wants to be the one to drive me into the ground? That's okay with me. I tell her that. She keeps asking me if I'm scared. Scared of what? Of her seeing me vulnerable? Broken? Will I be trapped in her spell? She says I'll fall in and not be able to untangle myself from her sticky web. She has no idea where I've been. Hell, I've been held prisoner by poisonous snakes. I've bled until there were no more tears. Love scars are sliced all over my breasts. I tell her that I am not afraid of her games nor where they lead.

"Ask around," I say. "Ask around about how I love."

"Then you're not afraid," she says more than asks.

I don't answer.

"I'm coming there. Right now, I'm coming there. Concentrate. Can you feel me in your room?"

I open my eyes the tiniest bit. The candle light seems to jump erratically on the walls. Have I left a window cracked? Is she in the room? Yes. Perhaps I am just the slightest bit afraid.

"Are you ready to play?"

"Yes," I whisper.

"Get out of bed."

I flip the blanket aside and stand barefoot on the carpet.

"We're going to a club in New York. Put on dance music."

I click on the CD player.

"I want you to dance in front of your closet mirror. Watch yourself move."

One minute in bed, the next I'm in front of the mirror. I sway to the music — oh yes, women like her know how easily I'm seduced. When the scene is played right, I'm a willing victim of circumstance. She knows this. She paints the backdrop with words. She creates the mood by murmuring vivid images across a telephone line.

"We're in New York. In a dance club. The place is packed. You dance alone by the mirror. Colored lights cut through the fog of the hazy dance floor. You dance. You dance. You dance. And then, as you move, you see me across the club, dressed in black and staring at you."

She pauses and I keep dancing.

"Like a daring hunter, I come toward you, through the thick-pressed crowd. The writhing dancers disintegrate into dreamy, shifting shadows. There is nothing but you and me. You stare at me. There is no one but me. Once I have caught your eye, there is no one else."

I gaze into my closet mirror and see her behind me. Dressed in black, she crosses the crowded dance floor. The dancers seem to fall aside as she advances. I see only her. There is no past. There is no future. All I have is the promise of what she brings with her, in this moment.

I feel immobilized, yet I'm certain that I'm still dancing to the driving beat. I turn to face her. The diamond stud in her lapel glitters and hypnotizes. I'm unable to pull my concentration from that sparkling stone. What she wants, I do not know. Something about hunger. It doesn't matter. I'm prepared to offer her whatever it is.

Her shoes shine with a black sheen. Her pants are sleek, her sport coat classic. She walks as if she's familiar with the night. The closer she comes, the clearer I am that she is no stranger to the dark.

I'm not afraid. I'm looking for an escort. I'm looking for someone to take my hand and drag me out of this club and into the alley.

She steps so close that I'm forced against the closet mirror. The glass is as cold as her eyes. She dances without touching me. Next to me, around me, through me. And then, in a breath we are in the alley.

She pushes me against the dirty building. Rough brick scrapes against my back. I like it. My dress is sheer and does little to protect me from the cold, from the harshness of the grimy wall. Her focus is direct. Her hands grasp my arms with firm intention. Her gaze burns a hole in the center of my being. What would fill that charred place if she were to leave?

She fondles my breasts and my nipples tighten in sweet response. *Oh please. Yes, please.* Her face is hard with icy desire. Her cold demeanor entrances me. *Love me but don't. Love me but don't.*

"Listen," she whispers in my ear. She bites my neck. "I'm going to have you right here against the wall. You will not speak. You will not make a sound. I'll have you against this wall and if you make one sound, I walk. I walk and I won't look back. Not once."

Her tone is harsh. Yes, I think. Take me. I can be the quietest girl. I'm so hot for her that I can barely stand. Her lips are warm against my ear. Her breath is steady. She pushes her body against mine. I have no place to go but further into the wall.

All I can imagine is the sensation of her fingers plunging into me. I hope my back is scratched. I want to look in the mirror tomorrow morning and see the marks that she's left.

She unzips the back of my dress and the silk cascades to my waist. My nipples are thick. My nipples are red stones. Her face is blank, vacant. I search her eyes for a glimpse of desire, a hint of heat. Nothing.

She grasps my nipples between her fingers. She twists them and the hurt feels good. I want to moan. My entire body has risen to a higher level of desire. My back stings and I squirm. She is tough, I like it.

She is rough, I need it. My sex dampens with delicious anticipation. *Okay, yes, okay, please.*

She goes too slow. She takes her time and I'm lost in unquenchable thirst. If only, if only she'd slip her fingers past my garters, beneath my panties and into me. I am so soft. I am so sweet. I know this. Each night, when I speak to her on the phone, I have my fingers in buried secret flesh.

And now, in a dream, she has brought me to this place. She crossed a midnight sky on a telephone wire, sliced through a crowded dance floor to take me to this alley. My back is pressed against the wall, I imagine the scrapes and want to plead with her to make me come.

"Stop squirming. Don't move," she mutters.

I go limp. Her unbending demeanor and the firm wall are all that keep me from slipping to the ground. If only she'd ... if only ...

"You want me to fuck you, little girl? Is that what the hunger is all about?" She buries her face in my hair. "Fuck you? Fuck you?"

I nod. I grasp her arms. Relief thunders through me. *Oh yes. Please.* All I want, all I need is the sensation of being emptied but filled, unsatisfied but pleased, abandoned but safe. *Love me hard, love me tender. Love me against a dirty brick wall. Take me without regard. Take me with complete awe.* Paradox. Paradox. I want it all.

She grabs me and pushes her cold hand up my dress. There is nothing in her eyes yet I can read the passion of a thousand suitors far beyond, deep in the center of her cavernous pupils. *I am no stranger*

*to the cold. I am no stranger to anguish, take me
there. I love it. I love you. I love it. I love you.*

She tugs my panties down. She's in a hurry now.
Good. So am I. We are running out of time. I could
fall out of this stupor at any minute. I could find
myself in my bedroom, pressed against the mirror,
telephone in hand.

Even though I'm creamy and drenched, it is still
an effort for her to go deep in her first, fast thrust.
Oh and oh. Oh and oh. She drives into me. My flesh
is raw against the bricks. My clit hangs low with
unstable desire. Rock-hard and ready.

An intensity sweeps through my body. I shudder
and call her name again and again.

She stops. She grabs my hair and jerks my head.
"I told you not to speak." She steps back. "I told you
not to speak."

Disoriented. Euphoric. I reach blindly for her. One
last step back and then she turns, walks the alley
and disappears around the corner.

I cover my breasts and hurry after her. "Wait!
Wait!"

I turn the corner. She is nowhere to be seen. The
street is dark and dangerous. Three men glance over
at me from a dingy front stoop.

"Looking for something, baby?" one calls in a low
voice.

No. I'm looking for nothing. I turn to escape. I
run down the alley — are they after me? Has she left
me stranded? The back door to the club is locked. I
hear them, their footsteps loud in the vacant alley.
Oh God. Has she left me?

"Are you frightened?" Her voice pulls me from the alley, back to the closet mirror.

I open my eyes. The candle flames skate on black pools of wax. I can barely breathe. My heart beats furiously. I feel shaken and drugged.

"Are you frightened?" she asks again.

"No. Not at all," I lie.

The dark goddess is somewhere in the shadows, calling to me.

"Tell me about the hunger." Her voice is steady, but I am certain of the reckless undertones.

Hanging onto the receiver for dear life, I slide against the cool mirror all the way to the floor.

What would fill that charred place if she were to leave?

SPONTANEOUS
COMBUSTION

.

Three nights later, I'm lying in bed, tired but awake. I've just awakened from a fleeting dream. About her? I can't be sure. The fragment is elusive. Even so, something about it, about her, soothes me. I linger in a misty haze and wonder.

It's barely after midnight and the house is dark. She's told me, when I miss her, to close my eyes and she'll ride to me on the midnight wind. She's in New York on business. It's after three there. I know she's lost in a deep sleep yet as I lie in bed, this intense wave of her enters the room. As if, even in her dreams, she can hear me and answer my call. I'm suddenly wired and sleepless. She's here? She's here? If the candles were lit, I'd surely see the flames yielding to her subtle breeze. A dim glow comes from the night light and nothing more. The only way to be certain that she's here is to believe.

Impossible. She's asleep in New York.

I fluff my pillows and try to shake my need for her. A growing disquiet lies next to me like a restless lover. Twelve-thirty. Twelve forty-five.

The ring of the phone startles me. Unexpected calls late at night frighten me. A crank call? An emergency? I wait for the second ring to pick up.

"Hello?" My heart races.

"I'm there with you. I've come to you on a midnight wind." Her tone is as seductive as a summer eve. Her voice thrills me — and I'm a dancer, pirouetting across a petal-covered floor. Her voice chills me — and I'm a diver, gliding through tropic blue. Her voice, her voice, her voice — I'm a girl whispering in Santa's ear; I'm a young woman flirting; I'm a siren enchanting. Her voice — and I'm everything.

"I can't believe you've called," I say quickly, as if any hesitation would steal her to the darkness. "I was lying here awake, on edge, wishing there was some way to reach you."

She laughs, a long, low laugh. "I told you, just close your eyes and I'm there."

"You are absolutely —"

"Tell me about the last time I called you," she interrupts. "Tell me about that." Her breath is steady, hypnotizing.

144

I close my eyes. I know what she wants. Our last phone conversation, she wove her sensual words into a beautiful tapestry. On magic-carpet images, she brought me to New York. Against a dirty brick wall in a back street alley, she fucked me with her words. I want her to ask again so I can hear the need in her voice.

"What exactly do you want to know?" I'm careful to let a shadowy innocence slither between my words.

Her breath accelerates slightly but she says nothing. I love how she refuses to surrender.

"How it was for me? Is that what you want?" I try to coax her to give in.

Silence.

She always pleases me. I'm more than happy to concede to her. I take in a long, slow breath and fall into the memory of last week's call. How I soared from my bed to a New York fantasy simply by riding her words. In an alley she took me, had me fast and hard. She did as she pleased.

"You found all these places in me that have never been exposed —"

In a midnight forest, a hazy silhouette of myself gathers twigs and sticks. I fill my arms with as much as I can and carry them to a circle of dirt surrounded by stones. I lay the sticks one by one in the center.

"You turned me inside out. Places not meant to be touched were electric under your caress. I was trembling. I was quivering. I was loose and tight, all at once. I was nothing and everything under your fingers —"

As I speak, I feel a silk cocoon enclosing me. When she calls me late at night, I lose myself in the rhythm of her breath.

I head back into the woods. I collect another armful of sticks and return to the pile. The air has a chill and I look forward to the heat.

"In an alley in New York, in your hands, I floated in sweet paradox. Without taking a single step, I tangoed across a ballroom floor. Because of you. You reached inside of me and pulled the dancer from deep within."

With her, in a New York dream, I had been all that I could be. Beneath the fiery tips of her fingers, I could barely stand. My legs were rubbery and weak, yet I was suspended in a cloud, a mist of pleasure.

"From a bedroom here, to an alley in New York, you had me. Exposed, opened, separated. Hungry and aching, I lay in bed. I fell in your arms. I was alone — with you all over me. On my breasts, in my sex. I was drenched with desire yet more arid than ever. Desperate to have my thirst quenched, I begged you."

I search the ground for fallen branches. Although it is pitch-black, I can still see my way. I bring more wood to the circle. Again more. And again.

The cadence of her breath entrances me and suddenly I'm back in the alley and under her spell.

"You spill a waterfall of slippery dew all over me.

I'm alone in bed and suddenly, without touching myself, I'm wet, wetter, soaked."

"I've got you pushed against the fire escape." Her words are lightning-charged. "I've got you pushed right there and I'm pressing into you. I'm staring in your eyes and I'm pressing as far in as I can go."

Am I awake or have I drifted into a trance? An unbroken circuit of energy rockets across the night from her to me. It zaps my erected nipples and zooms down into my slippery folds. I feel her in the room. I feel her on a New York fire escape. Her hands have found their way to my center of desire. Her words whip across my clit in rapid, fluttery strokes.

"I like it like that. Right there. Right there. Please, please, please, please. Right there. I like that."

She spins me like a yo-yo. In electric blues and purples, I swirl away. She lets me go yet holds me by a thin string, all the while.

"Baby, baby. Right, right there. Please, please, please."

Broken branches lie in a heap in the circle of stones. Cross-legged, I sit on the cold ground and stare at the pile of splintered limbs. Somewhere in a dream, she's touching me. She's opened my shirt, she's unhooked my lacy bra. Tiny sparks zip from her fingertips and sting my fever-pink nipples. The sensation is both bitter and sweet. I spread my legs open for her. I want her so bad.

I peer at the tangled kindling. She's behind me

now. Her breath is turbulent, stormy. Her fingernails dig into the flesh of my back. Her teeth bite into my neck.

"That's it, baby. That's it, girl." I'm muttering now. In bed, alone, I've jammed my fingers into my panties. Like a venomous snake's tongue, my finger lashes light and quick across my flappy clit. The gathering blood brings my conch-pink pussy to raw red. The folds swell. The once soft flesh is now hard and barely pliable.

"I've got you now." Her words flare. Blaze. Burn.

Her fingers find my raised nipples. Glints of orange shoot from my pebble-hard clit, across my belly and to my breasts. An endless progression of heat-waves crashes through me. Behind me, next to me, in front of me — she's everywhere. From her eyes, a single, focused beam of fiery light glows. As if following a razor-thin line of gasoline, a minute crimson flame dances on the ray that starts in her eyes and ends in mine.

She pinches both my nipples so hard that I gasp. An electrical storm builds in my body. With more pressure she plucks and twists, never once letting up. Snapping flames streak between us. I'm caught in an uncontrollable climb. A scorching intensity throbs in my clit in time with the pounding of my heart.

I am greasy wet. A glorious pleasure, a dangerous pleasure, rides me good. And the night is dark, the night is cold. She's on me now. She has me now. She pushes me to the hard forest floor and straddles my hips. Over me, down on me, she moves her hips like she's mounted a bounding steed. Go baby go. Go, baby, go.

Her hips are thunder. Under her, I'm riding each wild thrust. Flames leap from her eyes to mine. A laser light sears me. She's sucking my neck. She's leaving marks all over me, bruising me. The night air has thickened to a cold satin sheet. Blacker and blacker, darker and darker.

From her to me, the bolt streaks. She rides me like Zeus rides the sky, like Thor rides the clouds. Her pelvis against mine, her mound pressed to mine. A concentrated line of fire shoots from her to me. I'm jerking, I'm clinging to her for dear, dear life. On a burning pleasure, I glance to the circle of stones, to the intertwined wood and

    and

    and

a burst of flames roars — from her to me to the pile of wood. Oh my God, oh my God. Her tongue dabs my pussy. Her tongue separates the cleaves. She finds her target and zeroes in. The wood erupts in a fireball of heat. I'm holding fast to her. I'm going to ride this one to the very end. She drives me with her hips and I'm blasted from a volcano in a cloud of molten red heat.

Her words, her words her words —

"And with that I kiss you," she whispers. "I look deeply in your eyes and I see you. I see you there.

From three thousand miles away, I will touch you a thousand times like that and see everything about you."

If I open my eyes, I'm certain to find a ribbon of smoke still lingering above and ashes smeared across my breasts.

NOBODY'S FOOL

Friday night.

In front of my computer, I stare at the screen. I'm trying to write but all I can think of is you. The light from a single candle spills a golden glow across my desk. In a lazy spiral, a trail of incense smoke drifts toward the ceiling. A midnight-blue silk gown flows over my body like a soft curtain, to mid-calf. A single gold chain glistens on my neck. Except for spaghetti straps, my shoulders are bare. I feel elegant. I feel feminine. Scarlet red is thick on my lips. My eyes are Cleopatra-lined.

A liquid sapphire gown, a strand of gold and the swirl of rose petal scent is all I wear. I imagine you are coming to me. You are a thousand miles away, even so, I'm dressed and waiting for the thought of you to walk through the door.

Your lips warm on the nape of my neck, your whispered words in my ear — any moment now, you could arrive. I close my eyes and listen intently to the silence. If I concentrate, will I hear your breath? If I'm patient with the quiet, will you make your presence known?

The luxurious silk indulges my skin. Fingertips flutter across my neck and alight on one thin strap. Unhurried, they slide down my shoulder and dip into a sea of indigo silk. Eyes closed, waiting for you, I fall into sweet sensations as my hand follows the curve of my breast to my ready nipple.

And if you came through the door this very instant? A simmering silhouette of myself rises from the chair. The path to the door is as arid as a bone-dry stream. Victim of a jaded heart, knowing full well that I have wandered far too long in a merciless love drought, I hurry to see if you have come to my doorstep with a cache of rain.

I lean into the oak door. My breathing is quick. A swarm of butterflies somersaults in my belly. Ear flush against cold wood — yes, yes, I hear it. Subtle at first and then stronger, more forceful, heaving waves lap against the frame.

You have come to me.

Against the door yet spinning in a sparkling vortex in the room's center, I fluctuate between suspension and unending circles. A delicious dizziness overtakes me. Flashes of light seem to fly from me and ricochet from wall to wall. Again and again, I reel in imaginary rings. In a moon-goddess's ritual, I dance for your thunder. In an ancient ceremony, I call upon your storm to crash through the threshold. *Fill this desert heart.*

Unafraid, ready, I swing open the door. Intent and focused, the fantasy of you stands before me. With a wink of your eye, you hurl a harnessed gale into the room. Helpless, I slam against the wall. The harsh current wraps my elegant blue silk tight to my body. My hair is swept from my face. Your lips move but all I hear is a symphony of wind.

From your eyes, diamond slivers speed toward me like shimmering arrows straight from the twang of Cupid's bow. Grateful that my arms are confined to my side and my inherent compulsion to shield myself has been hampered, I bask in the hope that one, two — *however many barbed tips necessary* — will pierce my skin.

A romantic at heart, isn't that what you've called yourself?

"I'm coming after you," you promised. "I'm coming after you with a bouquet of dreams."

You stand in the doorway and a fierce excitement snaps between us. Pleasure crackles on my skin. You have that look in your eyes and I have no doubts about your intentions.

"You," you whisper. "You —" You point a single finger at me. "I'm coming after you like never before."

I can hardly stay standing — after all, since you, I've been on my knees. Since you, I've been weak with desire. You step into the room. The wind suddenly stops and the storm of who you are

153

drenches me. I crumple to the floor. My beautiful silk dress is soaked.

You glance at my gown and then back to my eyes. "Doesn't matter about the dress." You smile. The twinkle in your eyes reminds me of your rogue-like demeanor.

"It doesn't?" I pout — after all, I'm a femme. After all, this dress is my favorite.

You shake your head and from behind your back, you present me with a handful of blue-purple flowers. In slow motion, petals begin to fall from the blossoms. One, then two, they float to the floor and land in a puddle of inky blue.

The storm has passed and the room is suddenly quiet.

"I promise," you say without blinking an eye, "that I can weave these petals into a silk dress and more."

I open my eyes. The computer screen glares. My candle has extinguished itself and the room is dark. I don't want to write. All I want is you. I push from my desk and cross the room. A sharp edge scrapes at me. The phone sits quiet on the end table. Will you call tonight? Why didn't you call last night?

Restless, I peek between the curtains to the empty street. The moon has deserted the sky and a single star glints far away.

"Star bright, star light." I turn from the window and consider first star wishes. A concept fabricated by the dream-spinners?

I wish . . . I wish . . .

On the desk, the computer screen beckons. I'm empty of words. Depleted. I'm looking for something to fill me again.

"Like a heated waterfall, romance is going to pour thousands of words into you," you had insisted.

Friday night, dressed in blue silk, I'm thinking about romance and waiting for the promised words.

I wander the hallway to my room and automatically focus on the night stand phone. Why haven't you called?

A romantic at heart, that's what you said.

"Who cares about romance," I mutter. Nobody's fool, I call upon invisible walls to surround me with safety. Nobody's fool, I reach for the robe that hangs from the door — the robe you left last time you were here, the robe that still has the scent of you. Nobody's fool, I wrap the robe tight over my silk and head back to my desk.

The tapping sound is light. I stand in the room and stare at the door. Was it a knock? Is someone at the door?

"Who is it?" I whisper and step closer. "Who is it?"

"A romantic." Even through the door, your voice is strong and clear.

Not a dream, not a vision, you have really come to me. In an excited flurry, I open the door and fall into your embrace. No time for words, you lift me in your arms and carry me to bed. I'm kissing you. I'm kissing you again and again. All I can think of is how far you've traveled to surprise me.

We tumble into bed. From your pocket you pull a

handful of glittery rhinestone stars. "For you." You spill them across the bed and then kiss my hand. *A romantic at heart.* "All I want is you."

Self-imposed walls enclose me — even so, I long for you to push through this barricade into my callous heart. With the finesse of a magician, will you slip through? Unchain me? Use your pocketful of romance, your handful of stars to peel away this webbed cocoon?

Caught in the lover's contradiction of wanting you in yet keeping you out, easily deceived yet nobody's fool, I lament that I can't be broken. But your tempting words, *all I want is you,* delight me and I giggle anyway. After all, I can still relish the luxury of temporary respite.

"It pleases me that you're wearing my robe." You run your fingertip along the belt's knot. "Had you guessed I was coming?"

I shook my head. "Wished that you were."

You tug on the knotted sash while I lie still in heated anticipation. The robe slips from my shoulders. You lower the silk dress to my breasts, over my hips and down my legs. My nipples are hard. My sex is already damp.

"I like your dress." You glide the silk across my belly in slow circles. "Can I use your dress to bring you through the darkness to the light?"

I nod. On some level, I trust you implicitly.

You wrap the dress around my eyes and tie it like a large blindfold. I am suspended in a transitory moment. I'm submerged in an ocean of deep-sea silk. It's dark. You say you will bring me through to the light — is this like the promise of words?

I wear a silk-dress blindfold, a thin gold chain,

the scent of rose petals and nothing more. Under your guidance, I lean back in the bed.

"I believe in romance," you murmur. You kiss my neck, my shoulders, the slope of my breasts. "I believe in romance. I believe in romance. I believe in romance." Your words roll into each other in complete circles.

The gown is saturated with rose perfume. Have I been dropped into the center of a large, velvety rose? In the black of blind sensation, soft petals and sweet scents surround me.

"I believe in romance. I believe in romance. I believe in romance."

Your lips press on my belly and your lava-hot words creep down to the fringe of my sex hair, through the tangled corn-silk and slow, slow, slow into the grove between the lips.

"I have so many stars to scatter across your heart," you say and the tip of your tongue follows the trail of words toward my cloistered clit.

Nobody's fool, I spread my legs for you. Nobody's fool, I allow myself the splendor of temporary fantasy. *So many stars to scatter across your heart.*

Your tongue slices between the lips and flirts with my throbbing clitoral flesh. I know that I'm soaked, I know that I'm sticky.

"I believe in romance," you say. "I believe in romance." Your words are blasts of heat that swirl in the air.

I'm a slow-drifting glacier. Imprisoned in an icy shell, I want to stop you, to tell you that I've fallen for that illusion one time too many, yet I lie in silky darkness and hope that your sun-spun words will begin the long-awaited thaw. Your hands are warm on my belly. As much as I want to surrender, resisting is my only hope.

"I believe in romance," you say. "I believe in romance," you vow.

Even beneath this blindfold, there is no place to hide from the intensity of your words. Your tone is one born from a place of knowing — that place where iron and steel thoughts are coiled into rigid promises. Something about how you say it makes it hard not to believe.

Nobody's fool, I consider removing the blindfold. Nobody's fool, I try to remember the way out.

The tip of your tongue barely grazes my clit and we're suddenly connected by the most fragile link. I teeter on that cusp between you and me. Your tongue is light, light, light on my clit and the magician waves her wand.

"I believe in romance. I believe in romance."

Entombed in midnight silk, swallowed in the darkness, your liturgical chant begins to entrance. Do you have the key to this locked heart? Until this moment, I've been unable to melt. I've been hurt so badly that ice feels good and hard feels safe.

"I believe in romance," you say and your tongue slides further into my sex. I'm wetter than I can imagine. All I want is for you to push as far as you can into me. Will you? Will you invade, fearlessly — a warrior who will finally bring this tyrant ruler to her knees?

When romance slumbers in weary hibernation, winter is lonesome and bleak. My heart sleeps in a desolate den. A tangle of discarded dreams blocks the entrance. Have you come, machete in hand, to free me? Do you bring me one last chance?

Your tongue finds its way into the very heart of my being and I become an avalanche of snow, crashing from high above to a frozen sea. In a rush, every heartache I've endured tumbles in a mass of single snowflakes toward the ice-glazed sea. In the cold of a silk-blue ocean, down in the dark you have brought to me, I teeter on the edge of vacant hope.

"I believe in romance," you say and all I can do is dodge the snowslide. I think of who you are and how far you've journeyed. A pocketful of romance and a bouquet of dreams is what you've promised.

Nobody's fool, I understand how a woman's touch can bring me to my knees. Nobody's fool, I refuse to fall victim to the romance of sex. *Because she makes me climax, does not mean that I love her,* I remind myself again and again.

The dress covers my face and I'm hungry for air. If I decide to come out from the dark, will you be angry, take this as a sign that I simply can't succumb? Your tongue rides the sweetest place. If I rip the blindfold aside and breathe will you be disappointed?

You believe in romance
It's too dark under here.
You believe in romance
It's hard to breathe.
You believe in romance
I don't want to play anymore. It's safer the way it is. A jaded heart is an unscathed heart.

I can't stand it. I tear the dress from my eyes. The room is bright and you are lost somewhere between my legs. I grab your hair and pull your face from my treasures. Your mouth is rubbed red and milk-white sex glistens on your chin. The bed is covered with blue-purple petals. Rhinestone stars are scattered across my belly.

You peer directly into my eyes. "I believe in romance and I'm coming after you." You kiss your way up my belly, between my breasts, along my neck and then, your tender lips meet mine.

I sense your heartbeat. I hear your quiet breath. I lie calm yet deep inside, I rock like a buoy in a restless sea. Your embrace is as gentle as a flower petal floating down a stream. It's a cruel paradox — to be so close to you and so far away, simultaneously.

I waited at the computer, stared at the phone, peered out the window, longing for you. All I wanted was you. You came all this way with a pocketful of romance and a handful of stars. Didn't I pray for cupid's arrows to find their mark? Wasn't that less than an hour ago?

Love aims her bow and I duck and dodge. Walls go up. I'm ice and rock and can't be touched . . . or can I? I'm tired of resisting. What I've wanted all along is for someone to push me through to the other side. To make me want to try love one more time.

Your lips are soft against my ear. "I want you to trust me," you say. "Won't you give me a chance?"

Is this any different than any other time? What's to keep this porcelain heart from smashing to the floor in jagged pieces. Why aren't you afraid of bleeding? What do you know that I can't remember?

"I don't know," I say. A lone tear sneaks down my cheek. If I give in to a whim, to the momentary illusion that love is good, how much will I have to pay later?

"I only want to love you." You kiss the tear, then another and another.

Tears stream from my eyes although I barely breathe. I should get out of bed, wrap myself in a robe and walk, walk, walk as far as I can. But I don't move. I lie still while you kiss each tear away. Nobody's fool. I'm a glacier — slowly moving compacted ice but I'm crying and can't seem to stop.

And your words are warm and your promises are like rays of sun. This ice is cold and you're too far away and I hate this distance and I want the heat. I'm looking for something to fill me again.

And if I give you a chance, simply because I want to believe? If I give myself a chance, simply because ... the desert is arid and you bring the hope of rain.

ONCE BITTEN

I'm thinking about her. How it was before her and what is now. I was walking down a deserted street. I was alone, or was someone at my side? I can't remember. All I know is that one moment the street was empty, the next, she was in the distance leaning against a brick building staring at me.

I liked the way it felt. The possibility of pleasure and fear all mixed in one. She came from nowhere. The street was desolate and then it was filled with her. There was nothing but her.

I looked at the figure of her — slim, sleek, leaning

against the wall — waiting. I glanced over my shoulder. Were we alone? Hadn't someone been with me just seconds before?

I raised the collar on my jacket, as if this could protect me, shield me. Nothing behind me, nothing ahead except for her.

Her arms were at her sides. Her hands were tucked into her jacket pockets. She wore a hat low on her brow. The only sound was the click-clack of my shoes against the pavement as I walked toward her. I struggled with a hard urge to turn and hurry away and yet, there was something that compelled me to go forward, something that made me leery of turning my back for even a second.

"Hello?" I said as my approach closed the space between us. She said nothing, just raised her head enough for me to see her eyes. Her clear, intense eyes.

I smiled. I planned on not stopping, of walking past her and on down the street until I reached that safe place in life where turning back was no longer an option. But as I entered her shadow, she grabbed my arm.

"You," she hissed.

From her fingers, a severe coldness penetrated my jacket and headed up my arm like a careening bullet.

"Yes?" I stopped in front of her. Ordinarily I would have kept going. Ordinarily I would have run, run, run and not looked back.

Her complexion was pale. Her beady eyes seemed chiseled into her face. Thin, drawn — her lips were blood red.

"Yes?" I said again.

"I've been waiting for you." She glared at me. "I

waited, followed you from the dance club, hurried down a parallel street and cut over to here, to you."

"You were at the club?" I asked as if this information was in some way relevant. But it wasn't — after all, from that second on — all that mattered was now. All that mattered was how loud the push of my blood sounded. How rapid my heartbeat was. How dizzy and vacant I suddenly felt.

"And now I'm here, one step ahead of you." She released my arm. I felt the loss of her grip and stood, almost sullen, before her. I wanted her to pull me down the street and out of sight. If someone had been walking with me, if they had fallen behind would they soon turn the corner, would they come in-between and make this stranger disappear?

"And I'm not going anywhere," she said as if she knew my fears. "No one can make me disappear."

I glanced down the street. Was there a car? A place she could take me to?

"If you close your eyes and breathe, just breathe long and slow, I can take you somewhere far, far from here." She was almost whispering.

I had nothing to lose. I never have anything to lose, not really. I'm no stranger to things vanishing in the blink of an eye, I'm no stranger to hurt and betrayal. I peered into her face. Where we were heading, was there pain? Would I eventually drift away on a sea of tears?

She pulled me into the alcove. Her hand, tight on my wrist, felt good, felt complete. She could do whatever she wanted. I was open to being taken. I was opened to being scared and then rescued. Into the alcove and against the wall, she pushed into me. Her mouth found my neck, her teeth pinched the tender flesh. Would she bite me? Would she pierce into me and make me hers? This was okay with me. I longed to be owned. I longed to be transformed into a night-woman who fed solely on love. Would she bring home to me the heated fire of her blood-love?

Her teeth were on my neck. I closed my eyes and fell into a dark place. She had an energy that inspired me to climb in, to get in, to move in, to take whatever I could from her. With the promise of release, she overpowered me. I couldn't turn away, even if she had shoved me from her grip and said for me to go. She was a narcotic and there was nothing more mesmerizing than this moment in the alcove with her.

The language of love is cryptic and enigmatic. She whispered in my ear and tempted me in tongues I couldn't discern. I was drunk from her. I staggered in the rhythm of her murmured words. Her teeth bit into my flesh and I was shaken down to my soul.

A door in the alcove creaked open. She pulled me into a darkened hallway and raced with me, flew with me, up a flight of stairs, higher and higher away from the street, away from the alcove, away from anyone coming around a corner and making this disappear.

We were in a room and in a flash she was all over me. She was all over me and I was limp beneath her touch. My ears, my cheeks, my lips, my neck were covered with fast kisses, light kisses. Her hands plunged from my shoulders to my hips and my stomach dropped as if I had leapt from a precipice.

Her mouth covered mine and I was sucked into the power of her kiss. Her lips were velvet warmth. Against the door, in the corner of the room, her mouth on mine, we shared the same breath.

Her mystical scent wrapped round and round upon itself, enclosing me in an invisible spice and musk chamber. If she were to have stepped away, left me that very moment, I surely would have swaggered in a disoriented, perfume haze for hours. But she didn't. She didn't go anywhere. She stayed right with me, in the corner, against the door.

She pulled back and looked me in the eye. "I've waited for you," she said again.

Her deep-set eyes were dark with swirled mysteries. Afraid that I'd get lost in the labyrinth, I shifted my focus away from her intent stare. Her cheeks were sculptured porcelain. Beneath the hat, her hair barely covered her ears. A tattoo of a thin serpent snaked from the lobe of her ear down somewhere beneath her shirt collar.

She lightly ran her fingertip along the tattoo. "Power gained at the price of submission. Do you understand about that? Have you had a tattoo?" She grasped my upper arms. Her fingers seemed to dig through my jacket, my shirt and deep into my flesh.

I shook my head — *No, I didn't have a tattoo*—and then nodded. *Yes, I understood about submission.*

My heart began to race. Had I actually been walking with someone on the street? Was someone wondering where I had disappeared to? Would someone come through the alcove, race up the flights of steps, break into this room and save me from myself?

She clicked the lock on the door and led me into the heavy-curtained room. In the center, over a circular dining table, a bare yellow bulb hung from a cord. The room was canopied in a minimum of amber light. A long mirror hung on the opposing wall. Besides this, the room was empty.

She let go of my hand and tossed her hat across the room. Her jacket dropped to the floor. She unbuttoned her shirt. The serpent tattoo curved down to her rounded breast. I could do nothing but stare. My feet felt sucked into the floor. My arms seemed heavy. My breath was labored and deep.

She smiled and an impenetrable wildness filled the room. She was looking at me. She was looking at me and not turning away. She unsnapped her pants. They sagged to the floor in a crumpled pile. She was coming for me. She took a step. She was coming for me, closer, closer —

With nothing to lose, I let my jacket fall. No stranger to risk, I lifted my shirt. Did I understand about power? Did I know about letting go? No, but yes. No, but yes.

She was in front of me, her lips merely seconds from mine. I wanted the serpent to slither from her body to my neck, down my breast and at last, to my heart. Would stiletto fangs pierce the jaded, tough wall that caged my heart? God, I hoped so. I hoped so.

A stream of electric blue sizzled from her mouth to mine. Tiny zaps of power flashed. Her hand enclosed mine. Her lips trailed from my mouth, down my neck to my ready nipple. Against the table, onto the table, she guided me. The wood was cool against my back. She climbed on top of me. Her soft breasts

167

were plush against mine. Her belly on my belly. She grasped me, held me tight. A muffled, low cry came from deep inside of her. I arched beneath her. Butterflies fluttered from her to me. Musical notes looped up and around. Passion, like thick, melted metal, poured between us.

I closed my eyes, hoping, waiting for the moment when the serpent would find its way to my willing heart. "Yes, find me," I whispered.

She slid down between my legs. She turned so her sex was above my mouth and then, in a sweet second, her tongue cleaved my folds and delved into the soft until she found me.

Inches from my mouth, her dark-haired triangle teased. Her scent evoked such desire in me that I felt as if a volcanic push would throw us both off the table if I didn't submerge my face in the source.

Her mouth on my jewel, my mouth on hers. The flesh was slick, smooth, voluptuous. I felt as if I had dived into a vat of thick red jam. Her hands grabbed my ass. I cupped hers. I burrowed further into her cache. Her tongue whipped against my clit like a wave hard-crashing a single massive rock.

We shared one breath. We drank the paradise of each other's fluid. Slow, slow, slow. I began to feel the movement — subtle, but apparent just the same. My hands still on her ass, I clenched my fists in excited anticipation. It slid onto my thighs and then, smooth and cool, it undulated across my belly. Would it sting? Would I yell out when the fangs broke through the flesh. A puncture? A tear? A rip? Would I bleed? Would blood seep from the heart of me and soak the flesh between us? She'd slip and slide in the heated liquid, smearing who I am across us both.

She sucked my clit and exquisite pleasure filled me. I was scared but not. I had nothing to lose. But would it hurt? Would it drain me of everything I had?

Power gained at the price of submission.

Power gained at the price of submission.

The soul of me into her mouth. At my breast the energy coiled and hissed. I held my breath. I tightened in anticipation and fear. And then, with the fury of a long-denied lover, the serpent slashed into my heart.

I'm thinking about her. How it was before her and what it is now. There's something about surrender that brings us home to ourselves. The serpent's tail ends in its mouth and the circle becomes complete.

BREAKING AND ENTRY

There's this place that I wanted to go. There's this place, deep in the recesses of my heart that I craved being taken to. One sea-blown night off the Oregon coast, she looked me in the eyes and said she could take me there. Take me all the way there, down, down, down to the place where I was no longer bound, the place where I became free strictly by surrendering myself to someone else.

"I can take you there," she promised. "I can take you there." Her voice was low. Her voice was sultry. Her voice soothed me with the hope of release.

I wondered as we drove the dark windy roads of the Oregon coast if she would take me all the way to the haven of light or leave me stranded on a lonely road off the Oregon sea.

She's come to me in so many ways. She's listened to every word, every breath, every dream. With her, I've walked through my fears and whispered my truths. She looked at me and I capsized to my knees.

I consider how I love her. I consider how I wedded her in a ritual of tears.

She came to me on a windy night. My door was unlocked. I awaited her in a candlelit room. She promised she'd come to me and help me get there, to that place where I could love again.

Break me, come deep into me, then wrap around me and protect me from the pain.

I consider how afraid I'd been. Afraid of myself, afraid of my own numbness. She burned that out of me, sliced it out of me, exorcised it from me. Afraid of myself, I asked her to come to me with ice in her eyes. Afraid of myself, I asked her to force me into places from where I couldn't escape. Afraid of myself, I asked her to trap me in a chamber with myself.

She brought me to baths with petals and oils, caressed me with the sweetest words, pampered me with silk and gold and then, when she had me wrapped in her glittery spell, she cut to my core with stiletto words, drained the bath, pushed me away and ripped my silk.

With love, she brought me the coldness I desired. *Break me down to the smallest girl,* I pleaded, and she did.

I consider how I surrendered to her. How her sweet loving pulled me in, her hard loving netted me.

She held me hostage, I didn't care. Made it so I couldn't move. Made it so I was simply there until I wasn't.

She became all that I feared. She became all that I loved. Like a magician, she flashed her magic around the room and I was hypnotized by who she was. As sorceress, she snapped her fingers and I slammed to the floor in one fast blow.

I wanted so much to be broken. There was something about the pain that brought me home to the child inside who had cried forever. When she took me down, when I no longer had to hang onto myself, I could finally let go and explore all of the dark corners in my soul. When she broke me down, I was free to feel. I was free to let the avalanche of pain seep from me like sap.

I hid in a locked, darkened room. She stepped into the black and knelt before me. I was collapsed in the corner, crying tears from deep within and she handed me a box of beautiful silk. I consider how I simply succumbed.

I gave her an ivory heart. In a pouch in her pocket, she carried it wherever she went. I felt her fingers as she caressed the charm, felt the heat from her fingertips. I felt the dampness when she sweated, the chill when she was cold. A thousand miles and I rode in her pocket wherever she went. A thousand miles and not even an inch away. A thousand miles and she was in every breath I took.

She loved me, protected me, saved me, cared for me — and pushed me until I cried, cried. Pushed me until I finally returned to myself. As I hung on for dear life, she broke and entered only to lay a treasure-full of love at my feet.

It wasn't really a prince I'd been searching for all this time. The loneliness that haunted me for so long had been more an emptiness that came from within rather than without. I know this now. I waited for someone to whisk me into the sunset, but however far I went, the emptiness followed.

Through these three lovers, I began a journey into myself. The events that took me deeper and deeper were not about the women themselves, but more about my reaction to the circumstances that unfolded. The struggle became less about finding fulfillment *out there* and more about uncovering the prince within. Using my lovers as a vehicle rather than as the end themselves, I allowed myself the opportunity to let go. This was a surrender, through them, to myself.

I have a lover now. She lives far away. She comes to me and is gone, and even so, I feel complete. After all, with or without her, I have myself. This is the place that I've ultimately come to. By permitting myself to walk the dark, to let go, to surrender first to them and then to myself, I have come to a place so freeing, to a place so warm, that I finally have eluded the emptiness.

I'm my own lover now. Whoever comes into my life becomes an adjunct to this rather than the focus of it.

I'm my own lover now. A seasoned traveler. I've journeyed a beam of light out to the place where it pierces the dark. No stranger to risks, I've fought dragons and demons. I've leapt from precipices, crossed dry, cracked riverbeds and hurried down alleyways into the dark.

> She took my hand and helped me find my own
>   way into myself
> I'm my own lover now.
> Around a corner and up a flight of stairs, I
>   opened a door
> I'm my own lover now.
> There, in an otherwise empty room, I found a
>   vision of myself waiting patiently for my arrival.
> The image smiles.
> I'm a survivor
> From the dark to the light

From the dark to the light
I'm my own lover now.
The princess rides off into the sunrise.
Whether with or without her — I have myself.

I sit on the brink of the world and watch glorious dawn break through the night. I have come a long distance yet the road spans far beyond. In a temporary respite, I empty my satchel onto a silk cloth . . .

— A velvet pouch filled with rhinestone stars. I sprinkle them into my hand and flurry them over the edge.

— A kaleidoscope. I peer through the glass, out to the place where morning light fractures into a multitude of colors.

— A fountain pen filled with the possibility of glittery words.

And last, from the satchel, I pull my journal . . .

One moment I'm staring at an empty page
and the next, filled with visions
I'm sketching a dream

A few of the publications of
THE NAIAD PRESS, INC.
P.O. Box 10543 • Tallahassee, Florida 32302
Phone (904) 539-5965
Toll-Free Order Number: 1-800-533-1973
Mail orders welcome. Please include 15% postage.

THE BEACH AFFAIR by Barbara Johnson. 224 pp. Sizzling
summer romance/mystery/intrigue.   ISBN 1-56280-090-6 $10.95

GETTING THERE by Robbi Sommers. 192 pp. Nobody does it
like Robbi!   ISBN 1-56280-099-X   10.95

FINAL CUT by Lisa Haddock. 208 pp. 2nd Carmen Ramirez mystery.
                                             ISBN 1-56280-088-4   10.95

FLASHPOINT by Katherine V. Forrest. 256 pp. A Lesbian
blockbuster!   ISBN 1-56280-079-5   10.95

DAUGHTERS OF A CORAL DAWN by Katherine V. Forrest.
Audio Book — read by Jane Merrow.   ISBN 1-56280-110-4   16.95

CLAIRE OF THE MOON by Nicole Conn. Audio Book —Read
by Marianne Hyatt.   ISBN 1-56280-113-9   16.95

FOR LOVE AND FOR LIFE: INTIMATE PORTRAITS OF
LESBIAN COUPLES by Susan Johnson. 224 pp.
                                             ISBN 1-56280-091-4   14.95

DEVOTION by Mindy Kaplan. 192 pp. See the movie — read
the book!   ISBN 1-56280-093-0   10.95

SOMEONE TO WATCH by Jaye Maiman. 272 pp. A Robin Miller
mystery. 4th in a series.   ISBN 1-56280-095-7   10.95

GREENER THAN GRASS by Jennifer Fulton. 208 pp. A young
woman — a stranger in her bed.   ISBN 1-56280-092-2   10.95

TRAVELS WITH DIANA HUNTER by Regine Sands. Erotic
lesbian romp. Audio Book (2 cassettes)   ISBN 1-56280-107-4   16.95

CABIN FEVER by Carol Schmidt. 256 pp. Sizzling suspense
and passion.   ISBN 1-56280-089-1   10.95

THERE WILL BE NO GOODBYES by Laura DeHart Young. 192
pp. Romantic love, strength, and friendship. ISBN 1-56280-103-1   10.95

FAULTLINE by Sheila Ortiz Taylor. 144 pp. Joyous comic
lesbian novel.   ISBN 1-56280-108-2   9.95

OPEN HOUSE by Pat Welch. 176 pp. P.I. Helen Black's fourth
case.   ISBN 1-56280-102-3   10.95

ONCE MORE WITH FEELING by Peggy J. Herring. 240 pp.
Lighthearted, loving romantic adventure.   ISBN 1-56280-089-2   10.95

FOREVER by Evelyn Kennedy. 224 pp. Passionate romance — love
overcoming all obstacles.   ISBN 1-56280-094-9   10.95

WHISPERS by Kris Bruyer. 176 pp. Romantic ghost story
                                             ISBN 1-56280-082-5   10.95

NIGHT SONGS by Penny Mickelbury. 224 pp. A Gianna
Maglione Mystery. Second in a series.   ISBN 1-56280-097-3   10.95

GETTING TO THE POINT by Teresa Stores. 256 pp. Classic
southern Lesbian novel.   ISBN 1-56280-100-7   10.95

PAINTED MOON by Karin Kallmaker. 224 pp. Delicious
Kallmaker romance.   ISBN 1-56280-075-2   10.95

THE MYSTERIOUS NAIAD edited by Katherine V. Forrest &
Barbara Grier. 320 pp. Love stories by Naiad Press authors.
                                             ISBN 1-56280-074-4   14.95

DAUGHTERS OF A CORAL DAWN by Katherine V. Forrest.
240 pp. Tenth Anniversay Edition.   ISBN 1-56280-104-X   10.95

BODY GUARD by Claire McNab. 208 pp. A Carol Ashton Mystery.
6th in a series.   ISBN 1-56280-073-6   10.95

CACTUS LOVE by Lee Lynch. 192 pp. Stories by the beloved
storyteller.   ISBN 1-56280-071-X   9.95

SECOND GUESS by Rose Beecham. 216 pp. An Amanda Valentine
Mystery. 2nd in a series.   ISBN 1-56280-069-8   9.95

THE SURE THING by Melissa Hartman. 208 pp. L.A. earthquake
romance.   ISBN 1-56280-078-7   9.95

A RAGE OF MAIDENS by Lauren Wright Douglas. 240 pp. A
Caitlin Reece Mystery. 6th in a series.   ISBN 1-56280-068-X   10.95

TRIPLE EXPOSURE by Jackie Calhoun. 224 pp. Romantic drama
involving many characters.   ISBN 1-56280-067-1   9.95

UP, UP AND AWAY by Catherine Ennis. 192 pp. Delightful
romance.   ISBN 1-56280-065-5   9.95

PERSONAL ADS by Robbi Sommers. 176 pp. Sizzling short
stories.   ISBN 1-56280-059-0   9.95

FLASHPOINT by Katherine V. Forrest. 256 pp. Lesbian
blockbuster!   ISBN 1-56280-043-4   22.95

CROSSWORDS by Penny Sumner. 256 pp. 2nd Victoria Cross
Mystery.   ISBN 1-56280-064-7   9.95

SWEET CHERRY WINE by Carol Schmidt. 224 pp. A novel of
suspense.   ISBN 1-56280-063-9   9.95

CERTAIN SMILES by Dorothy Tell. 160 pp. Erotic short stories.
                                             ISBN 1-56280-066-3   9.95

EDITED OUT by Lisa Haddock. 224 pp. 1st Carmen Ramirez
Mystery. ISBN 1-56280-077-9   9.95

WEDNESDAY NIGHTS by Camarin Grae. 288 pp. Sexy
adventure. ISBN 1-56280-060-4   10.95

SMOKEY O by Celia Cohen. 176 pp. Relationships on the
playing field. ISBN 1-56280-057-4   9.95

KATHLEEN O'DONALD by Penny Hayes. 256 pp. Rose and
Kathleen find each other and employment in 1909 NYC.
ISBN 1-56280-070-1   9.95

STAYING HOME by Elisabeth Nonas. 256 pp. Molly and Alix
want a baby . . . or do they? ISBN 1-56280-076-0   10.95

TRUE LOVE by Jennifer Fulton. 240 pp. Six lesbians searching
for love in all the "right" places. ISBN 1-56280-035-3   10.95

GARDENIAS WHERE THERE ARE NONE by Molleen Zanger.
176 pp. Why is Melanie inextricably drawn to the old house?
ISBN 1-56280-056-6   9.95

KEEPING SECRETS by Penny Mickelbury. 208 pp. A Gianna
Maglione Mystery. First in a series. ISBN 1-56280-052-3   9.95

THE ROMANTIC NAIAD edited by Katherine V. Forrest &
Barbara Grier. 336 pp. Love stories by Naiad Press authors.
ISBN 1-56280-054-X   14.95

UNDER MY SKIN by Jaye Maiman. 336 pp. A Robin Miller
mystery. 3rd in a series. ISBN 1-56280-049-3.   10.95

STAY TOONED by Rhonda Dicksion. 144 pp. Cartoons — 1st
collection since *Lesbian Survival Manual.* ISBN 1-56280-045-0   9.95

CAR POOL by Karin Kallmaker. 272pp. Lesbians on wheels
and then some! ISBN 1-56280-048-5   10.95

NOT TELLING MOTHER: STORIES FROM A LIFE by Diane
Salvatore. 176 pp. Her 3rd novel. ISBN 1-56280-044-2   9.95

GOBLIN MARKET by Lauren Wright Douglas. 240pp. A Caitlin
Reece Mystery. 5th in a series. ISBN 1-56280-047-7   10.95

LONG GOODBYES by Nikki Baker. 256 pp. A Virginia Kelly
mystery. 3rd in a series. ISBN 1-56280-042-6   9.95

FRIENDS AND LOVERS by Jackie Calhoun. 224 pp. Mid-western
Lesbian lives and loves. ISBN 1-56280-041-8   10.95

THE CAT CAME BACK by Hilary Mullins. 208 pp. Highly
praised Lesbian novel. ISBN 1-56280-040-X   9.95

BEHIND CLOSED DOORS by Robbi Sommers. 192 pp. Hot,
erotic short stories. ISBN 1-56280-039-6   9.95

CLAIRE OF THE MOON by Nicole Conn. 192 pp. See the
movie — read the book! ISBN 1-56280-038-8   10.95

SILENT HEART by Claire McNab. 192 pp. Exotic Lesbian
romance. ISBN 1-56280-036-1   10.95

HAPPY ENDINGS by Kate Brandt. 272 pp. Intimate conversations
with Lesbian authors. ISBN 1-56280-050-7   10.95

THE SPY IN QUESTION by Amanda Kyle Williams. 256 pp.
4th Madison McGuire. ISBN 1-56280-037-X   9.95

SAVING GRACE by Jennifer Fulton. 240 pp. Adventure and
romantic entanglement. ISBN 1-56280-051-5   9.95

THE YEAR SEVEN by Molleen Zanger. 208 pp. Women surviving
in a new world. ISBN 1-56280-034-5   9.95

CURIOUS WINE by Katherine V. Forrest. 176 pp. Tenth Anniver-
sary Edition. The most popular contemporary Lesbian love story.
ISBN 1-56280-053-1   10.95
    Audio Book (2 cassettes) ISBN 1-56280-105-8   16.95

CHAUTAUQUA by Catherine Ennis. 192 pp. Exciting, romantic
adventure. ISBN 1-56280-032-9   9.95

A PROPER BURIAL by Pat Welch. 192 pp. A Helen Black
mystery. 3rd in a series. ISBN 1-56280-033-7   9.95

SILVERLAKE HEAT: A Novel of Suspense by Carol Schmidt.
240 pp. Rhonda is as hot as Laney's dreams. ISBN 1-56280-031-0   9.95

LOVE, ZENA BETH by Diane Salvatore. 224 pp. The most talked
about lesbian novel of the nineties! ISBN 1-56280-030-2   10.95

A DOORYARD FULL OF FLOWERS by Isabel Miller. 160 pp.
Stories incl. 2 sequels to *Patience and Sarah.*   ISBN 1-56280-029-9   9.95

MURDER BY TRADITION by Katherine V. Forrest. 288 pp. A
Kate Delafield Mystery. 4th in a series. ISBN 1-56280-002-7   10.95

THE EROTIC NAIAD edited by Katherine V. Forrest & Barbara
Grier. 224 pp. Love stories by Naiad Press authors.
ISBN 1-56280-026-4   13.95

DEAD CERTAIN by Claire McNab. 224 pp. A Carol Ashton
mystery. 5th in a series. ISBN 1-56280-027-2   9.95

CRAZY FOR LOVING by Jaye Maiman. 320 pp. A Robin Miller
mystery. 2nd in a series. ISBN 1-56280-025-6   9.95

STONEHURST by Barbara Johnson. 176 pp. Passionate regency
romance. ISBN 1-56280-024-8   10.95

INTRODUCING AMANDA VALENTINE by Rose Beecham.
256 pp. An Amanda Valentine Mystery. First in a series.
ISBN 1-56280-021-3   9.95

UNCERTAIN COMPANIONS by Robbi Sommers. 204 pp.
Steamy, erotic novel. ISBN 1-56280-017-5   9.95

A TIGER'S HEART by Lauren W. Douglas. 240 pp. A Caitlin
Reece mystery. 4th in a series. ISBN 1-56280-018-3   9.95

PAPERBACK ROMANCE by Karin Kallmaker. 256 pp. A
delicious romance.   ISBN 1-56280-019-1   9.95

MORTON RIVER VALLEY by Lee Lynch. 304 pp. Lee Lynch
at her best!   ISBN 1-56280-016-7   9.95

THE LAVENDER HOUSE MURDER by Nikki Baker. 224 pp.
A Virginia Kelly Mystery. 2nd in a series.   ISBN 1-56280-012-4   9.95

PASSION BAY by Jennifer Fulton. 224 pp. Passionate romance,
virgin beaches, tropical skies.   ISBN 1-56280-028-0   10.95

STICKS AND STONES by Jackie Calhoun. 208 pp. Contemporary
lesbian lives and loves.   ISBN 1-56280-020-5   9.95
Audio Book (2 cassettes)   ISBN 1-56280-106-6   16.95

DELIA IRONFOOT by Jeane Harris. 192 pp. Adventure for Delia
and Beth in the Utah mountains.   ISBN 1-56280-014-0   9.95

UNDER THE SOUTHERN CROSS by Claire McNab. 192 pp.
Romantic nights Down Under.   ISBN 1-56280-011-6   9.95

GRASSY FLATS by Penny Hayes. 256 pp. Lesbian romance in
the '30s.   ISBN 1-56280-010-8   9.95

A SINGULAR SPY by Amanda K. Williams. 192 pp. 3rd
Madison McGuire.   ISBN 1-56280-008-6   8.95

THE END OF APRIL by Penny Sumner. 240 pp. A Victoria
Cross mystery. First in a series.   ISBN 1-56280-007-8   8.95

HOUSTON TOWN by Deborah Powell. 208 pp. A Hollis
Carpenter mystery.   ISBN 1-56280-006-X   8.95

KISS AND TELL by Robbi Sommers. 192 pp. Scorching stories
by the author of *Pleasures*.   ISBN 1-56280-005-1   10.95

STILL WATERS by Pat Welch. 208 pp. A Helen Black mystery.
2nd in a series.   ISBN 0-941483-97-5   9.95

TO LOVE AGAIN by Evelyn Kennedy. 208 pp. Wildly romantic
love story.   ISBN 0-941483-85-1   9.95

IN THE GAME by Nikki Baker. 192 pp. A Virginia Kelly
mystery. First in a series.   ISBN 1-56280-004-3   9.95

AVALON by Mary Jane Jones. 256 pp. A Lesbian Arthurian
romance.   ISBN 0-941483-96-7   9.95

STRANDED by Camarin Grae. 320 pp. Entertaining, riveting
adventure.   ISBN 0-941483-99-1   9.95

THE DAUGHTERS OF ARTEMIS by Lauren Wright Douglas.
240 pp. A Caitlin Reece mystery. 3rd in a series.
                                      ISBN 0-941483-95-9   9.95

CLEARWATER by Catherine Ennis. 176 pp. Romantic secrets
of a small Louisiana town.   ISBN 0-941483-65-7   8.95

THE HALLELUJAH MURDERS by Dorothy Tell. 176 pp. A
Poppy Dillworth mystery. 2nd in a series.   ISBN 0-941483-88-6   8.95

SECOND CHANCE by Jackie Calhoun. 256 pp. Contemporary
Lesbian lives and loves.   ISBN 0-941483-93-2   9.95

BENEDICTION by Diane Salvatore. 272 pp. Striking, contemporary romantic novel.   ISBN 0-941483-90-8   9.95

BLACK IRIS by Jeane Harris. 192 pp. Caroline's hidden past . . .
                                       ISBN 0-941483-68-1   8.95

TOUCHWOOD by Karin Kallmaker. 240 pp. Loving, May/
December romance.   ISBN 0-941483-76-2   9.95

COP OUT by Claire McNab. 208 pp. A Carol Ashton mystery.
4th in a series.   ISBN 0-941483-84-3   9.95

THE BEVERLY MALIBU by Katherine V. Forrest. 288 pp. A
Kate Delafield Mystery. 3rd in a series.   ISBN 0-941483-48-7   10.95

THAT OLD STUDEBAKER by Lee Lynch. 272 pp. Andy's affair
with Regina and her attachment to her beloved car.
                                       ISBN 0-941483-82-7   9.95

PASSION'S LEGACY by Lori Paige. 224 pp. Sarah is swept into
the arms of Augusta Pym in this delightful historical romance.
                                       ISBN 0-941483-81-9   8.95

THE PROVIDENCE FILE by Amanda Kyle Williams. 256 pp.
Second Madison McGuire   ISBN 0-941483-92-4   8.95

I LEFT MY HEART by Jaye Maiman. 320 pp. A Robin Miller
Mystery. First in a series.   ISBN 0-941483-72-X   10.95

THE PRICE OF SALT by Patricia Highsmith (writing as Claire
Morgan). 288 pp. Classic lesbian novel, first issued in 1952 . . .
acknowledged by its author under her own, very famous, name.
                                       ISBN 1-56280-003-5   9.95

SIDE BY SIDE by Isabel Miller. 256 pp. From beloved author of
Patience and Sarah.   ISBN 0-941483-77-0   9.95

STAYING POWER: LONG TERM LESBIAN COUPLES by
Susan E. Johnson. 352 pp. Joys of coupledom. ISBN 0-941-483-75-4 14.95

SLICK by Camarin Grae. 304 pp. Exotic, erotic adventure.
                                       ISBN 0-941483-74-6   9.95

NINTH LIFE by Lauren Wright Douglas. 256 pp. A Caitlin Reece
mystery. 2nd in a series.   ISBN 0-941483-50-9   8.95

PLAYERS by Robbi Sommers. 192 pp. Sizzling, erotic novel.
                                       ISBN 0-941483-73-8   9.95

MURDER AT RED ROOK RANCH by Dorothy Tell. 224 pp.
A Poppy Dillworth mystery. 1st in a series.   ISBN 0-941483-80-0   8.95

LESBIAN SURVIVAL MANUAL by Rhonda Dicksion. 112 pp.
Cartoons!   ISBN 0-941483-71-1   8.95

A ROOM FULL OF WOMEN by Elisabeth Nonas. 256 pp.
Contemporary Lesbian lives.   ISBN 0-941483-69-X   9.95

THEME FOR DIVERSE INSTRUMENTS by Jane Rule. 208 pp.
Powerful romantic lesbian stories.   ISBN 0-941483-63-0   8.95
CLUB 12 by Amanda Kyle Williams. 288 pp. Espionage thriller
featuring a lesbian agent!   ISBN 0-941483-64-9   8.95
DEATH DOWN UNDER by Claire McNab. 240 pp. A Carol
Ashton mystery. 3rd in a series.   ISBN 0-941483-39-8   9.95
MONTANA FEATHERS by Penny Hayes. 256 pp. Vivian and
Elizabeth find love in frontier Montana.   ISBN 0-941483-61-4   8.95
LIFESTYLES by Jackie Calhoun. 224 pp. Contemporary Lesbian
lives and loves.   ISBN 0-941483-57-6   9.95
WILDERNESS TREK by Dorothy Tell. 192 pp. Six women on
vacation learning "new" skills.   ISBN 0-941483-60-6   8.95
MURDER BY THE BOOK by Pat Welch. 256 pp. A Helen Black
Mystery. First in a series.   ISBN 0-941483-59-2   9.95
THERE'S SOMETHING I'VE BEEN MEANING TO TELL YOU
Ed. by Loralee MacPike. 288 pp. Gay men and lesbians coming out
to their children.   ISBN 0-941483-44-4   9.95
LIFTING BELLY by Gertrude Stein. Ed. by Rebecca Mark. 104 pp.
Erotic poetry.   ISBN 0-941483-51-7   10.95
AFTER THE FIRE by Jane Rule. 256 pp. Warm, human novel by
this incomparable author.   ISBN 0-941483-45-2   8.95
THREE WOMEN by March Hastings. 232 pp. Golden oldie. A
triangle among wealthy sophisticates.   ISBN 0-941483-43-6   8.95
PLEASURES by Robbi Sommers. 204 pp. Unprecedented
eroticism.   ISBN 0-941483-49-5   8.95
EDGEWISE by Camarin Grae. 372 pp. Spellbinding
adventure.   ISBN 0-941483-19-3   9.95
FATAL REUNION by Claire McNab. 224 pp. A Carol Ashton
mystery. 2nd in a series.   ISBN 0-941483-40-1   8.95
IN EVERY PORT by Karin Kallmaker. 228 pp. Jessica's sexy,
adventuresome travels.   ISBN 0-941483-37-7   9.95
OF LOVE AND GLORY by Evelyn Kennedy. 192 pp. Exciting
WWII romance.   ISBN 0-941483-32-0   8.95
CLICKING STONES by Nancy Tyler Glenn. 288 pp. Love
transcending time.   ISBN 0-941483-31-2   9.95
SOUTH OF THE LINE by Catherine Ennis. 216 pp. Civil War
adventure.   ISBN 0-941483-29-0   8.95

These are just a few of the many Naiad Press titles — we are the oldest and
largest lesbian/feminist publishing company in the world. Please request a
complete catalog. We offer personal service; we encourage and welcome
direct mail orders from individuals who have limited access to bookstores
carrying our publications.